He couldn't think of anything he wanted more than for Jasmine to spend the rest of the night with him.

"Need to go?" he finally asked.

Jasmine hesitated. If he'd been in her situation, he would have, too.

Covering the few steps left between them, Royce let his body act on instinct. He reached out and cupped the cool skin of her upper arms. Then he rubbed up and down, aiming to warm her. But also to fulfill his own craving to simply touch her.

She stared up at him in the dark. Beneath his touch, she shivered, then she shook her head no.

"Then come back to bed."

That first touch of skin on skin exhilarated him. He rolled over her in the bed, covering her cool body with his warmth. Savoring the gasp of air that signaled her surrender.

A Family
for the Billionaire

DANI WADE

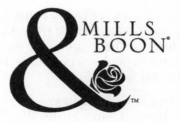

First published in Great Britain 2017
By Mills & Boon, an imprint of HarperCollins*Publishers*
1 London Bridge Street, London, SE1 9GF

Large Print edition 2017

© 2017 Katherine Worsham

ISBN: 978-0-263-07217-4

Printed and bound in Great Britain
by CPI Antony Rowe, Chippenham, Wiltshire

Dani Wade astonished her local librarians as a teenager when she carried home ten books every week—and actually read them all. Now she writes her own characters, who clamor for attention in the midst of the chaos that is her life. Residing in the Southern United States with a husband, two kids, two dogs and one grumpy cat, she stays busy until she can closet herself away with her characters once more.

To all the sisters
who have enriched my travels and
blessed my life—LeaAnn, Sheridan,
Tammy, Hannah, Nicole, Kim, Kira,
Andrea, Marilyn, Linda and LJ.

My journeys
wouldn't have been the same without you…

One

"I assume this meeting is being conducted with the utmost confidentiality?"

"Of course," Jasmine Harden said, though she had never before had to assure a potential client of that.

"Then I'll be honest."

She eyed Royce Brazier as he paced before her in his suit and tie. The floor-to-ceiling windows of his office overlooked the river and provided the perfect backdrop. Gorgeous—the man and the view. As he paused for a moment, she noticed just a hint of something on his neck, right above his collar in the back. Was that a tattoo?

Quickly Jasmine dropped her gaze. She knew exactly how easy it was to read her expression, so she turned her thoughts in more businesslike directions.

"Besides," he continued as he faced her once more, "if word got out, I'd know where it came from, wouldn't I?"

Okay, Royce was making it a lot easier to focus on business.

"My shipping fleet has done very well, but I'm interested in taking my business to a new level. To that end, I'm aiming to attract a certain family that I hope will contract extensive work from my fleet." A frown marred Royce's smooth forehead. She could almost see the thoughts as they took hold of him. "This family is very altruistic and so I want to do a fund-raising event that appeals to them."

"So this is all about a business deal?" Though she could understand the logic Royce was working with, the conclusion was still disappointing. The hot CEO apparently didn't have a heart...

"It's purely a business endeavor. As with other projects, I'll write the check, you do the work."

Wasn't that a nice attitude? Not. Though

Jasmine regularly worked with high-profile businessmen in this city, she'd never had one approach her with a proposal this cold. "Why me?" she asked quietly.

"I did my research," he said, turning a direct stare on her that made her uncomfortably aware of things other than business. "You're well known in the circles I want to attract, your clients have a very high rate of satisfaction and we use some of the same vendors, the best vendors in the city of Savannah."

His praise should make her feel better, right?

"My assistant received some wonderful feedback on you. You were rated the highest of star-quality event planners in the region.

"I only work with the best of the best. That's how I can trust you to do the work."

Why did he have to be so handsome? A handsome automaton. That slight peek at a tattoo on his neck had led her to expect more. A huff of laughter escaped as she imagined him as a true robot in her overactive imagination.

"Is there a problem?" he asked, narrowing his eyes on her as if suspicious she was making fun of him.

"Nothing." At least she hadn't giggled. That would definitely be unprofessional. "Can you tell me what charity you have in mind?" she asked, trying to get back on track.

"I don't. Pick whatever you feel is appropriate."

Jasmine blinked. Everything about this meeting was completely out of the ordinary when it came to how she worked with her clients.

"I simply need an event that is noteworthy and appropriate," he continued. "They seem to be involved in quite a few causes. Oh, and I need it in less than two months."

Oh, my. "So you think I'm a miracle worker?"

This time he relented enough to offer a small smile. "I certainly hope so. Otherwise the event will be too late to have any impact on my bid. Can I count on you?"

She thought back over their conversation. No. No. And no. "Listen, I don't think I'm the right person for this job." Or quite frankly, for this boss. She had a feeling that working for him would be a minefield, and with her life in tumult already, she didn't need a difficult boss.

He stopped his pacing to stare. "Why not?"

You're too handsome, too business minded and too cavalier about this endeavor altogether.

Only she couldn't say any of that out loud. Questions rang in Jasmine's mind as she watched him, thinking hard. She'd heard plenty about Royce Brazier, but she'd never actually met him before today, despite her extensive work with Savannah's elite. One of the city's youngest billionaires—self-made through his dedication to his quickly growing shipping business—he attended only a few select events on the social scene. Considering his reputation as a hard-nosed, focused businessman and what she'd seen during this meeting, she had a feeling he only did that much to maintain his business contacts.

His presence was commanding, his look suave and professional. So suave she wanted to mess with his perfectly placed blond hair just for the heck of it. Jasmine was professional, too, but she often had the feeling she was herding cats—especially since the arrival of Rosie...and often feared that it showed.

"Look," she tried to explain, searching for words that Royce would understand. "I realize charity events are good ways of getting positive press and word of mouth, but my events are known for having heart."

"Good. Then you can give a heart to mine."

She was still unsure how to make him understand that this wasn't a good fit for her. To her relief, his phone rang.

"Yes, Matthew?" he asked over the speaker.

"I'm sorry to bother you, sir, but your lawyer just had the agreement you requested delivered."

"I need to take a quick look at this," Royce explained to Jasmine. "Excuse me a moment."

"No problem." A few minutes to herself might give her time to regroup.

Glancing around his office, Jasmine noticed right off that there were no personal touches. No novels or magazines. No photographs of his family...or even of him with friends. A framed photo of a large building graced a prominent spot on the wall.

Jasmine couldn't imagine being this impersonal. She knew a lot of people, cared about a lot of people, but her family was her core support. Few others got to see behind her public persona. After losing her parents when she was a teenager, she couldn't imagine the devastation she would feel if she lost any other members of her family.

She'd known Royce wanted an event planned—after all, that's what she did. But his complete lack of personal interest or passion was daunting. And though there were some charities that didn't require the benefactor to be very involved, it wasn't the way she wanted to work.

But how could she convince him that a more hands-on approach was needed?

"So what do you say?" The smooth smile on Royce's face as he returned to the room was so attractive it made her chest ache. She saw a lot of powerful, pretty men in her job, but Royce had to be the pinnacle. Frankly, she wasn't sure what to do with that, either.

"Should we start talking contracts?"

Jasmine nodded, willing her expression to remain neutral. "Yes, but I have a few requirements of my own."

Royce Brazier eyed the woman before him with concern itching at his brain, though he was too smart to let it show.

Jasmine didn't seem like the bargaining type.

She appeared to be nothing like the cutthroat business people he dealt with on a daily basis. So why did he detect a hint of steel in those cornflower-blue eyes?

"A bit unusual for the event planner to start making demands, isn't it?"

She arched her brow in a challenging expression, but judging from the way she was tightly clasping her hands in her lap, he had a feeling it was false bravado.

"It's definitely not my normal MO," she said. "But a girl's got to have standards."

No apology—he liked that. "Name your price."

"Oh, it's not about price." She paused for a moment as she studied him. "It's about participation."

Royce was so caught up in her beauty that he wasn't getting all the cues. "I'm not following..."

"I'll happily take on your event—I already have some great ideas. And don't get me wrong. Being given a lot of freedom is an event planner's dream. But as I said, I have certain standards. This isn't about what's easiest for me...or you. A contract will require you to participate in each step of the process—"

"I guess we could touch base via phone." Though seeing her wouldn't be a hardship. Those blue eyes and her delicate bone structure were the first things to distract Royce from his business in a long, long time.

"You will participate by attending all the meetings that I deem necessary with vendors and representatives of the charity we support."

What? Hold on a minute. "Nice try, sweetheart. I have a business to run. And more than enough to do. That's why I'm hiring someone else to do this."

"I also have a business to run. And a reputation to protect. You need to be involved for this to work. So it's my way or no way."

Royce scrambled to figure out just what was going on here. "There's plenty of other event planners in this city."

Jasmine nodded graciously, but he again got the feeling there was steel behind the genteel smile. "And you're welcome to contact any of them, but they won't have the experience *I* have with your target audience." All too soon she was up and across the room, but she paused by the door. How could just the way she glanced back at him be so sexy? Especially as she proceeded to drop a bombshell. "I would like to remind you that I do know the Jeffersons personally, and I am a frequent guest at their parties."

Shock rocketed through him. How had she known?

"You *were* referring to the Jeffersons, weren't you? I do my homework, too."

As she strode out the door with a tempting flash of leg, Royce was impressed even though he knew he shouldn't be. *Sexy and smart.* It gave her too much of an advantage.

Two

"He knew exactly what he wanted," Jasmine told her sisters, "and he wasn't backing down."

"He's never come up against you before," Willow said with a grin. Jasmine's middle sister was a tenacious Southern woman, with the temper to match her copper-colored hair. Jasmine possessed a core of the same stuff but it only made a quiet appearance when necessary. She wouldn't scream and cry, but she didn't give up until every hope had been squashed flat by a steel-toed boot.

She might look like a lady, but she had more strength than most men. The tragedies in her life had demanded it. "Well, I believe I left him with some food for thought."

"So, you were wearing your blue dress?"

Jasmine frowned. Her sister's guess hit a little too close to home. "I didn't wear the dress to entice him. It's perfectly presentable."

Her sisters shared a grin. Jasmine tried to let it go. After all, she knew more than most that a little cleavage helped smooth the path she traveled. She'd be a fool not to take advantage of her God-given assets—especially when they'd helped her put both of her little sisters through college—in a completely respectable manner.

"Well, maybe the dress helped a little…" she admitted in a low voice as Auntie stepped into the kitchen with Rosie. The sight of her adopted daughter, and being surrounded by the people who meant the most to her in the world, filled Jasmine's heart and pushed aside thoughts of today's tedious meeting.

She reached out for six-month-old Rosie. She was in her snuggly jammies, her skin lavender-scented from her bath. As she settled into Jasmine's lap, Jasmine breathed deep. "I love you, baby girl," she whispered against Rosie's curly black hair.

Then she smiled up at the older woman. "Thank you, Auntie."

"You're most welcome," Auntie said, bending to hug Jasmine and the baby together.

Jasmine would never have made it through the first six months of Rosie's life without Auntie. Technically, she wasn't their aunt. She'd been their mother's nanny when she'd been small. She'd returned to Savannah when their mother hadn't needed her anymore.

But when the girls' parents had died, leaving them with no family at a very young age, Auntie had brought them home to Savannah. Jasmine had been a young teen, but her sisters were even younger. Auntie had finished raising them in this house and never once complained. She was as close to a mother as she could get without being a blood relation.

Each of the girls loved her just the same.

Jasmine's baby sister, Ivy, joined them at the table with a plate of oatmeal cookies Auntie had made while they were all at work that day. "I've seen Royce Brazier at some of the meetings of the transportation planning commission, since he owns one of the biggest shipping companies on the East Coast," she said, her bright blue eyes wide. "He's pretty hunky."

Jasmine could practically see every set of ears around the table perk up.

Ivy continued, "But I've heard he's all business, 24/7."

Jasmine agreed. "He made that very clear."

Willow pouted. "What's the fun in that?"

"Dealing with demands is a lot easier when they're pretty," Ivy said, with a grimace that still managed to look cute.

Jasmine threw her napkin across the table at her sister, making a sleepy Rosie giggle.

"The last thing I have time for right now is a man," Jasmine insisted.

Her cell phone gave a quiet chirp, which was the ringtone she used at home so she didn't accidentally wake the baby. She glanced at the screen. "He certainly is a workaholic," she mused as she handed Rosie over to her youngest sister. She hadn't expected to see Royce's name on the caller ID at this time of night—or at all, really. She'd assumed he would never go for her conditions. Which had made her sad, because she could have used the work. But she had her principles.

She needed to remember that.

"This is Jasmine," she answered, walking toward the door to the front parlor as her sisters mimed something and Auntie watched them indulgently.

"Brazier here."

She smiled. *I know.* "What can I do for you?"

"After careful consideration, I've decided to renegotiate our terms, if that's still possible."

Interesting. "May I ask why?"

"Well, you certainly have a lot to offer."

Was she just imagining his voice growing deeper?

He went on. "So I'll agree to your terms—within reason."

"Meaning?"

"I'll attend meetings with the charity and vendors and such, but I'm not decorating rooms or tying bows or stuffing bags. Understood?"

Good thing he couldn't see her smile. "Feel free to email me your demands and I'll consider them."

"You can't talk now?" he asked.

"Roy—Mr. Brazier. It's a little late. Almost nine o'clock." And Rosie would need to go to sleep soon.

"Is your husband impatient for you to get off the phone?"

Okay, no way had she imagined that change in tone. Choosing to ignore his question, because it was fun to keep him guessing, she countered, "Don't you have a family waiting for you to shut down?"

"No. A man with my schedule shouldn't have a family—it isn't fair to them."

She thought of the little girl in the other room—how sometimes it was hard to force herself out the door in the morning because being away from Rosie left her feeling incomplete. Of course, life hadn't afforded her the chance to stay home with Rosie—and there were plenty of family members in the house to keep her occupied until Mommy came home. "Commendable of you to realize that." Though most men usually didn't think that way.

"Simply practical—but you didn't answer my question."

And she didn't plan to… "Working 24/7 isn't good for anyone."

"You enjoy your beauty sleep?"

This conversation was definitely off the business track—her brain derailed into forbidden thoughts of him in her bed. "I'll watch for your email," she said, hoping she didn't sound too breathless.

She disconnected and returned to the other room. Her sisters were silent until she tried to pass, then they started in.

"Oh, Royce," Ivy said, gasping with an extra dash of drama. "I must, simply must, have your email."

"Is your wife waiting for you to get off the phone?" Willow teased.

"He asked first," Jasmine protested.

"Which just gave you permission to dig."

"It's a business deal." Why did she have a feeling she was trying to convince herself?

"It doesn't have to be," Auntie said as Jasmine lifted a sleeping Rosie into her arms.

Jasmine lowered her voice. "Not you, too, Auntie."

"Your mother would not want you to be alone."

The sisters froze at Auntie's words. She rarely butted into their personal lives; though she was free with her help and guidance, her one very short marriage hadn't qualified her to give advice to the lovelorn—according to her. So this was rare.

"I'm not," Jasmine insisted. "I have you, the girls, Rosie. What do I need a man for?"

"I love the little one, too, and all you girls," Auntie said. "But you keep yourself tucked away, protected. Your mother, despite everything she lost, still pushed forward and allowed love in. She would want that for all of you."

Jasmine studied her sisters, who looked at each other slightly abashed. Theirs was a tight circle, and other than casual dates in high school and college, no man had ever infiltrated it. No man had even come home for dinner. And the sisters had always lived together, even through college.

They were their own island oasis. The thought of that changing sent a streak of unease through Jasmine.

As if reading her mind, Auntie nodded at her. "Keeping your circle small is not going to protect you from pain, Jasmine." She smiled sadly. "It's time, my sweets."

"For what?" Willow asked when no one else would.

Jasmine didn't want to know. Rosie was all the change she could handle in her safe little world. Her only challenges were in her career and she preferred to keep it that way. But when Auntie spoke in that all-knowing voice, things usually happened. Whether anyone wanted them to or not.

The older woman got up and crossed to the door. Jasmine could hear her progress up the stairs and eventually back down in the historic, but sturdy, home. Auntie came straight to Jasmine, leaving her with the feeling she'd been found by an unerringly accurate arrow.

Dropping into the chair next to her, Auntie held out a small jeweler's box. Willow and Ivy leaned across the table for a better look.

"Your mother wanted you girls to have this," Auntie said as she opened the box. "I found it with her things, packed away with a letter."

Inside lay a ring with a teardrop-shaped emerald stone surrounded by decorative gold filigree. They all gasped—Jasmine included. It was an involuntary reflex. The ring was gorgeous. Not only that, it seemed to have something... something special that Jasmine couldn't quite put her finger on.

"Wait!" Willow said. "I remember Mama wearing that—she said it was an heirloom or something..."

"Indeed," Auntie confirmed. "It was passed down to her from her mother, who received it from her mother, and so on."

Jasmine stared at the beautiful jewel, a sudden memory of it on her mother's hand filling her mind. Her mother had been dressed up. An anniversary dinner, maybe? She and their father hadn't ever gone to fancy parties and such. About as fancy as it got was her father's Christmas gathering for the professors at the university where he taught. But she remembered her mother letting her stroke one small finger over the emerald. What had she said?

Then Auntie spoke, "Legend has it—"

Willow squealed. Jasmine groaned. Auntie gave them both an indulgent smile. Willow was the resident myth and legend hunter. She'd truly followed in their father's footsteps, teaching history at the local community college. She loved tall tales, mysteries and spooky stories. She propped her chin on her palm, avidly awaiting Auntie's words.

Jasmine just shook her head.

"Legend has it," Auntie started again, "that this ring was given to the woman who founded your family line by the man she married."

"Here in Savannah?" Ivy asked.

"Oh, yes. He was a pirate, you see, and she was the beautiful but shy daughter of a prominent family here."

Jasmine had tried hard to forget that their family had once been wealthy and respected. Long before the scandal that had rocked their safe little world.

Auntie went on. "He didn't think he had any chance to catch her eye, so he simply admired her from afar. But on his travels, he came into possession of this ring. He was told by the old man he bought it from that the ring would bring the person who owned it true love."

"Ooh," Willow said, her grin growing bigger and bigger.

"Sure enough, he was able to win his woman's hand…and the ring has been passed down to every generation of your family ever since. Each has claimed its power is real."

Ever the skeptic, Jasmine couldn't help but add, "And look how that worked for them. Scandals, death. Our family has some of the worst luck ever."

When Ivy's hopeful expression fell, it made Jasmine feel like a big bully.

"It's said to bring its owner true love, not an easy life," Auntie gently admonished, ever the voice of wisdom. "Besides, if the scandal hadn't driven your grandparents out of Savannah, then your mother and father might never have met."

Jasmine didn't want to disrespect the memory of her parents, but… "A ring did not cause them to find each other—being in the same place at the same time did."

"Maybe so—"

"Don't be a realist, Jasmine," Willow complained. "Embrace the magic."

Ivy reached over to take the sleeping baby and snuggled her close. Rosie gave a shuddering sigh. "Is it really healthy to teach Rosie that there's no magic, no romance in the world?"

"She's only six months old," Jasmine protested. "Besides, I didn't say that—" Jasmine created magic every day with her events, or rather, the *feeling* of magic.

Willow added her two cents' worth, even though Jasmine considered her biased. "Yeah, Jasmine, haven't you ever heard of Cinderella? Rapunzel? Beauty? Wendy? Dorothy?"

"You want me to convince Rosie there's magic in the world by indulging this nonsense and snaring a man?"

"No—the man is just a bonus," Ivy said with a giggle.

"An uptight CEO?" Jasmine couldn't believe she was hearing this.

Ivy wasn't deterred. "The uptight CEO with thick hair, muscular build and a tight a—"

Willow gasped and covered the sleeping baby's ears. "Ivy!"

Ivy grimaced. "But yes—that is a bonus. You just need to sweeten him up a little."

"For Rosie?"

"Yes!" her sisters said in unison.

"She needs a man around," Ivy went on. "After all, we didn't have one. How can we possibly teach her anything about men?"

They all paused, silently weighing the loss of their father. The only man they could remember being part of their family...and that was a long, long time ago.

Auntie finally weighed in. "She's already going to hear enough reality when she gets older and learns what happened to her birth mother," she reminded Jasmine with a sad look.

"Or are you just afraid the ring will actually work?" Willow jumped in.

Was she? Jasmine secretly admitted that all the loss she'd suffered in her young life made her reluctant to let someone else in. Only dire circumstances had brought Rosie to her. Jasmine had adopted her as a newborn at the behest of the little girl's dying mother. A woman Jasmine had come to know at the City Sanctuary mission where she'd volunteered—and then lost when Rosie's mother succumbed to the cancer she'd never been able to afford to have treated properly.

"The ring is for all of you girls, but I think

Jasmine has a unique opportunity here to prove her point...or ours." Auntie held out the ring box once more, smiling as if she understood Jasmine's dilemma all too well. "A little magic never hurt anyone," she said.

Somehow, Jasmine didn't believe that.

Three

So much for that businesslike attitude. Jasmine tapped her stiletto heel as she glanced at her watch once more. *He's twenty minutes late.*

She knew traffic hadn't held him up. The coffee shop she'd chosen for her brainstorming meeting with Royce was right near his office building. As she watched the boats on the river and the tourists wander by on the sidewalk, she struggled with her impatience.

Yes, something probably came up: a business call, papers to sign, something.

But why hadn't someone called? She'd sent the

contract in plenty of time. Her racing thoughts were driving her crazy.

I'll wait ten more minutes.

Just sitting here was annoying her all the more, so she dumped her coffee and set off toward his office building.

The gorgeous architecture and sweet smell of pralines from a riverside candy shop didn't calm her agitation as she walked over the stone pathways. Tension built up inside—a problem she'd never had with her clients. What was it about this guy? Usually she could just breathe and reroute her focus to where it needed to go in order to produce forward momentum toward their mutual goals.

Not today.

Days spent wondering what that tattoo was on his neck, whether his hair was mussed when he rolled out of bed in the morning or if he ever did anything but work had taken her to places she hadn't wanted to go. And the stupid ring wasn't helping.

She glanced down at the emerald she wasn't used to having on her right hand. So stupid. But if she backed down now, her sisters would never let her hear the end of it. So she'd prove to them that the legend wasn't real—and teach Rosie there were plenty of special things in life without magic.

Her phone started vibrating in her hand. Glancing down, Jasmine mumbled under her breath, "Well, it's about time."

"Hello, Mr. Brazier," she said.

His tone was as clipped as hers. "I need to postpone. Please come to my office in an hour." He was so short, she wondered if he even realized he was talking to an actual person.

"Excuse me?"

"Come here in an hour," he repeated.

Click.

An hour? Jasmine paused to scroll through the calendar on her phone. *Oh, my.* Since Royce had only allotted an hour for their meeting, Jasmine hadn't worried about the tight timeline she had for this morning. An hour would put her right smack in the middle of Auntie's doctor's appointment. Willow was in class. Ivy was at work. Which left…well, no one to watch Rosie. Except her.

He probably wasn't going to like how that

went… But then again, he hadn't really given her much choice in the matter. It was time Mr. Brazier got his first lesson in seeing the person behind the business opportunity.

When Jasmine walked into the outer office a little over an hour later, Matthew's eyes widened. "Miss Harden, I'm so sorry." His eyes widened further—if that was even possible—as he glanced down. "I—"

"Just announce me, please, Matthew," she said with an overly sweet smile.

Her stomach fluttered from the nerves rushing through her in waves, but she reminded herself necessity took this out of her hands. Besides, he'd brought it on himself.

Jasmine went through the door while Royce continued to talk on the phone. His back was to her. Taking advantage of his distraction, she turned and smiled down at her surprise. Then she lifted Rosie from her stroller and turned to find Royce staring at her backside.

Jasmine should have been offended, but his distraction played to her advantage in this instance. When he finally realized where he was staring and looked up, the switch from lust to shock in his normally schooled expression was priceless.

"What's this?" he sputtered as he jumped to his feet.

Jasmine ignored Rosie's cooing, because breaking her businesslike facade wouldn't be to her advantage right now. "You told me to meet you here."

He frowned, proving himself to be heartless. No one could look at Rosie and refuse to smile. No way could he be human. "My office isn't a day care," he insisted.

"And my time is very tightly scheduled today," she said with an arch of her brows. "I have commitments, just like you."

"I can't help that my earlier meeting ran over," he said defensively, straightening in his seat.

Jasmine took a deep breath, then blew it out slowly, pulling her chaotic thoughts from the last hour together. "Let me ask you a question," she began.

After Royce nodded, she continued. "Would you have called any of your fellow businessmen and given them commands about when to show up at your office?"

The surprise on his face only confirmed her suspicions.

"If I were one of your managers or the owner of one of your supply companies instead of an event planner, would you have had Matt contact me to reschedule instead of rudely cutting off our conversation earlier?"

"That's not why—"

"I made arrangements for a sitter as soon as this meeting was scheduled. I don't like to disrupt my daughter's schedule by carting her around to my business meetings. But by changing our scheduled time and refusing to discuss it with me or give me any options, I had no other choice…unless I wanted to be a no-show myself."

He didn't respond. His narrowed gaze still made her want to squirm, but she refused to back down.

"Now I'm very much looking forward to working with you, but my business is people. Is our phone conversation earlier how you conduct business? How you deal with your fellow business people and the community at large? Because it isn't how I conduct my business."

Lesson number one was over. The ball was in Royce's court now.

Rosie continued to coo, then snuggled against Jasmine as she settled into a chair with her child in her lap. This would never have worked if Rosie had a different temperament, but Jasmine happened to know that her daughter was one of the most easygoing babies in the world. She just hoped this was Royce's only lesson in seeing the people behind the business.

"If that's going to be a problem," she said, "then I release you from your contract right now."

He glanced back and forth between her and Rosie, as if he still couldn't catch the connection between his earlier behavior and having a baby in his office. But then he slowly shook his head. "No. I don't want to cancel our contract."

She wanted to ask why, but figured she'd pushed her luck enough for today.

"Maybe we should reschedule?" Royce said, staring down at them with a frown.

"Why?" Jasmine asked. "I'm here now. Your schedule appears to be free at the moment, which it hasn't been for the last two weeks. Let's talk."

When he hesitated, she prompted. "If we don't

get started soon, we'll miss your window of opportunity. I can't work miracles in two months. And neither can the vendors I hire."

Royce's careful expression returned as he took his seat. "I've found most people have a price that will motivate them."

"And that's the difference between the two of us."

Surprise momentarily replaced his serious expression. "What do you mean by that?"

"Just that I prefer to endear myself to people," she said, keeping her tone even and calm, not accusing. "I find they're much more willing to work hard, which makes life easier and the results quicker, if I'm nice."

"As opposed to employing coercion?" His smirk reminded her of exactly how they'd gotten into this situation.

"Sometimes other tactics are necessary," she conceded, "but it definitely makes things messy and uncomfortable for everyone. Confrontation might be a necessity at times, but I don't like it."

They shared a look of mutual understanding. Royce agreed with a nod. "But it is interesting."

Interesting, indeed.

* * *

Royce studied the woman in front of him, carefully avoiding looking at the raven-haired child in her lap. The sight of the little girl in his office brought too many mixed emotions.

He'd never been so far off his game that he wasn't sure where to begin...until this moment. But he wasn't about to let Jasmine Harden know that. She was proving her point...he wasn't about to help her.

For a moment, he second-guessed his decision to continue with this conversation. Heck, this whole project. But it wasn't just her connection to the Jeffersons that kept him from calling a halt right now.

Deep down, as uncomfortable as this entire incident made him, his instincts told him a woman who was this passionate about people was perfect to create the event that would connect him to others who were just as passionate.

"So, what do you have for me?" he finally asked.

The twitch of her lips suggested she knew exactly how uncomfortable he was. She shifted the baby into the crook of her arm with the ease of an earth mother, despite her power suit, and started her pitch.

"I want to do a masquerade."

Masquerade? "Like a dance?"

A half smile formed on her elegant red lips. Why did they have to be shaped so perfectly? He'd promised himself he would keep his thoughts on business…not on the woman. And he'd succeeded until the minute he'd seen her in person again.

Then she'd had to insist on him seeing her as a person. This wasn't helping him with his perspective at all.

"Sort of. A masquerade includes dancing. The key focus is the anonymity. Each participant wears a mask, which lends itself to a mysterious atmosphere."

"Isn't the point for people to know me?" He had to admit, he wasn't an imaginative kind of guy. At least, not in this area. Give him a logistics problem with his shipping company and his brain went into overdrive. Fantasy? Not really.

"Oh, they will," she assured him. "There will be announcements throughout the evening of the money being raised so everyone will be aware of the sponsor. But for the *participants*, the atmosphere is key."

She reached into her oversize bag to pull out a tablet. Flipping the cover open, she deftly pulled up what she was looking for. "As you can see, this gives us a theme to work with—a theme our target audience will find very attractive."

Without missing a beat, she set the device upright on his desk and flipped through pictures on the screen of lavish decorations and food and costumes. The only thing Royce saw were dollar signs.

"This looks awfully expensive."

Jasmine raised her brows at him. "Is money a problem?"

How could she make him feel like a schoolboy with a single look? "It isn't unlimited," he insisted.

"I wouldn't think so, but you said you wanted to make an impression."

Royce studied the last photo. A woman in a fitted dress and feather mask was laughing up at a man in a black tux. The woman's dark hair reminded him of Jasmine's... No—she was an employee. An employee with a baby.

Totally off limits.

"Why can't we just do a dinner?" he asked.

Of course, she had to counter with, "Why would anyone want to come?"

He studied the picture, realizing how totally out of his element he was. Maybe she'd been right to get him more involved. He had no idea how to attract people to anything other than a business deal.

"The draw at a charitable event isn't even the charity," she said, "which is a shame, but true."

A shuffling sound had him looking up. The baby's chubby cheeks and pale round face surrounded by a halo of inky black hair made her look like a cherub. She stared at him with her eyelids at half mast, thumb firmly held between her lips. When had the cooing stopped?

Jasmine leaned over to reach into the back of the stroller. When she straightened, she held a bottle that the baby eagerly reached for. Royce couldn't help but notice that there wasn't a ring on Jasmine's ring finger. No wedding band? He should have been even more upset by this situation, given his own childhood. Instead, a relief he was ashamed of snaked through him.

The fact that she was available shouldn't matter to him.

Settling back into the chair, Jasmine cuddled the sleepy child against her chest. The juxtaposition of working woman and mother unsettled him. His own mother had never seemed that at ease. Royce had always felt like he hindered her work whenever he was around.

"People want to be entertained," Jasmine said. "You have to sell an experience in order to get people to show up and spend their money. Build something that intrigues them and they'll tell all their friends and soon you'll have people begging for tickets."

The brief flicker of her thick lashes as she looked down at the dozing child in her lap had him holding his breath until she looked back up. But then she narrowed her gaze on him, giving him the uncomfortable feeling that she saw more than he wanted her to. "The more people who talk about wanting to attend, the more likely the buzz will get back to the Jeffersons. The name connected to the event matches the name on the newest bid they received. Mission accomplished—or at least you'll have made progress."

Royce was far more comfortable talking strategy than entertainment. "I wondered how we would make that connection."

She seemed to pull the baby a touch closer in her arms. He didn't want to notice, didn't want to think about the child. Royce had never attended a business meeting that gave rise to this many emotions—unease, lust, surprise, irritation. How long until this meeting was over?

"Besides being the talk of the town?" she asked. Her smile turned as mysterious as the woman in the photograph. "I may have a few tricks up my sleeve. After all, we need to get the word out in certain circles…so I thought I would use a few exclusive invitations I receive to introduce you around, talk it up."

"You want me to make social appearances… with you?" As if social appearances weren't awkward enough for him.

She nodded. "Including at the Jeffersons' Sunday Salon."

"You get invited?" So, she hadn't been exaggerating when she'd claimed a connection.

"About every other month."

The Sunday Salon was a coveted invite that

didn't come around that often for most people. The Jeffersons must adore Jasmine Harden, which told Royce he'd made the right choice of event planner—even if he didn't feel all that comfortable with it.

"All right," he said. "Tell me more."

He couldn't complain that Jasmine wasn't thorough. In ten minutes, he knew more than he really wanted to, but he had no doubt she was the best woman for the job. Before she finished he was convinced she would oversee every detail and nothing would be missed. She addressed every aspect of the planning, including quite a few things he never would have thought about.

"So what do you think?" she asked.

A lot of things he couldn't say at the moment— because they were completely unbusinesslike. Luckily she wasn't looking at him as she efficiently laid the baby down in the stroller. Was it terrible of him that he didn't know the child's name and was afraid to ask?

"Sounds good," he said, eager to be away from all the churning thoughts this meeting had raised. "Send the mock-up and budget projections to Matthew. Let me know when you need me for anything."

Her brows rose at his short tone, but she didn't question him. "I'll do that." She gathered her bag and tablet, then faced him once more. "When you look at the budget, remember that successful events involve getting all the details right, and that takes a lot of people."

"While logically I understand that—" and he truly was getting on board with the concept "—I still have to look at the bottom line."

Jasmine stared at him a moment; he detected the barest hint of an eye roll before her thick lashes swooped down. "Let's put it this way—is the time and money worth it to gain the new contract?"

Her words registered, but instead of thinking about business, Royce found himself holding his breath, waiting to see if she would look back up and show him those intense blue eyes once more. Then the baby let out a big sigh and broke the spell.

As Jasmine leaned over to look into the stroller, he forcibly pulled himself back to reality—and the knowledge that this woman was off limits in more ways than one.

"Yes, it is," he said. "You may proceed."

"Okay—we will need to start with the charity."

"I've told you it doesn't matter to me. Pick whatever you want."

"I have. You'll be helping raise money for a new building for the City Sanctuary homeless mission."

Royce nodded even as he tuned her out—though it wasn't as easy as he would have liked. He didn't care about the details—didn't want to care. He also didn't want to care about her thick hair and expressive face or the curves highlighted by the black power suit she wore.

"Also, we need to pick a venue right away. What dates would work for viewing possible locations?"

Her sharpened tone caused Royce to snap back to attention. She hadn't been kidding about the participation thing. Her long stare reinforced her message.

"Check with Matthew. He'll know what's available."

Smartly she stood up and pointed the stroller toward the door.

Royce had the sudden conviction that he couldn't let her walk out the door without making himself clear, as well. "I realize my point of view isn't a popular one these days, but as the child of a hardworking single mother myself, I have a strong opinion about children in the workplace," he said.

Glancing back at him, she asked, "What's that?"

"My office isn't a day care but I do apologize for my rudeness on the phone."

She gifted him with a sexy smile that had no place in his office, as much as he wished it did. But then came the sass. "Remember that and we will work together just fine."

Before he could respond, she pushed the stroller out the door. He heard her tell Matthew goodbye with that same sweet tone—this time with no steel undercurrents. She was definitely infuriating and intriguing.

Thoroughly dangerous territory.

Four

He'd thought about not showing up at all.

Staring up at the austere lines of the museum Jasmine had chosen as a possible venue, he wished he had ditched their meeting. But standing her up again was not a good option. She'd taught him that much.

Besides, his mama would have considered it ungentlemanly to simply ditch her—even if memories of his mama were what made him not want to show up at the museum in the first place.

But he had to stand firm. Today, he would take back the reins because he would not hold his event in a building he could no longer set foot in—much less play host in for an evening.

He was still staring at the building when Jasmine pulled up beside him in a pristine compact sedan. After climbing out, she smiled at him.

"Well, look at you," she said, her voice as teasing as it had been that first night on the phone when he'd called her. He didn't like to acknowledge the tingles of anticipation that hit him when he heard it—which were just as strong this morning as they had been then.

"I was a little unsure that you'd actually show up," she went on, "much less arrive early."

The tingle of anticipation grew, only this time it was for the challenge he knew was ahead of him. Still he struggled to keep any emotion from his expression.

"There's no point in going inside," he said, letting his tone match what he hoped was his deadpan expression.

Her frown as she shut the door and walked around the front of her car warned him that she was thinking hard about this turn of events. "May I ask why?"

"We aren't having my event here."

She glanced back over her shoulder at the building behind her, the multiple columns ma-

jestically holding up the austere gabled roof with
its carved marble depiction of birds. When she
turned to him, confusion reigned in those gorgeous blue eyes. "Again, may I ask why?"

"I don't want it here." And he didn't. No need
for discussion about his troubled childhood or
dead mother. "Personal reasons."

"Are they good enough reasons?" she asked,
tossing her hair over her shoulder.

"It is when I'm signing the checks."

Her expression told him she wanted to be
offended, even when she knew he was right.
But she wasn't simply accepting his decree. "I
thought you didn't want to be involved in the
decisions?" she demanded.

This wasn't the same as dealing with any of
his other business associates. When they slapped
their hands to their hips, he never noticed the
sway of their breasts. He shouldn't be noticing
Jasmine's now, but somehow he couldn't help
himself.

"And you said you wanted me to be involved in
making the decisions," he reminded her. "Which
is it?"

That little intake of air pushed her breasts out just a touch more. Heaven help him.

She nodded. He could tell she wanted further explanation. He wasn't giving it.

Finally she turned away, giving him a break from that penetrating gaze. "Let me go touch base with the manager," she said. "I need to stay on good terms here."

"Of course."

"Then we'll talk," she warned. Her heels clicked on the sidewalk as she strode away.

He waited until she went inside the museum before pulling out his phone. "Hey, Joseph," he said when his construction manager picked up. "How are things looking today?"

Joseph filled him in on the details of the kitchen installation at Royce's supersecret project, as well as other aspects of the restoration.

"Another day on track," Joseph confirmed.

"Good."

Royce hung up, a spur-of-the-moment idea buzzing in his brain. He had the lucky ability to run through all the immediate pros and cons of a decision in a relatively short amount of time. This had helped him jump on opportunities that other businesses spent months preparing for. Along with his intense drive, he'd used this to build his business to magnificent proportions at a very young age.

Today this ability would certainly come in handy.

He waited until Jasmine returned down the walk fifteen minutes later. His relief at finally being able to leave the site of one of his most traumatic childhood experiences was tempered with his desire to covertly take her in.

Jasmine seemed to enjoy ultrafeminine clothing. Even when she'd had the baby with her, she'd been wearing a women's business suit with a skirt and an undershirt with lace lining the deep V of the collar. Today, the bodice of her navy dress hugged curves that he normally wouldn't notice. But on her they made his mouth water. An inverted triangle cut out over her cleavage added to the effect. The flowing skirt that ended right below her knees revealed just enough of her legs to be tantalizing.

Was she trying to torture him?

"All done," she said as she approached. "What now?"

Oh, she was gonna love this. "I have an alternative. Let's go."

"Now?" Her frown was back.

"No time like the present. I'll drive."

But as they settled into the small space of his luxury sedan and the dark, sexy scent of her snuck up on him, he had to wonder whether he had made a wise choice.

Or was this self-sabotage?

Of all the things Jasmine had expected to do today, riding in the front seat of Royce's car was not one of them. The smooth, heavy scent of well-cared-for leather and a slight hint of aftershave teased her senses, making her notice things she wished she didn't.

This is business. This is business.

"Why don't you have a driver?" she asked, letting the first question that occurred to her pop out in an awkward attempt at conversation.

He glanced her way before returning his attention to the road. "That's a rather pretentious question, don't you think?"

"Actually it's simple curiosity that springs from experience," she corrected. "I've worked with a lot of Savannah's upper class. Most have their own drivers—at least, under certain circumstances."

The road was familiar to her from having lived in Savannah since she was fifteen years old. Though a lot of fine old houses could be found in the surrounding areas, she couldn't think of any in this particular direction. Where was he taking her?

She tempered her curiosity with more questions about his driverless state. If she had to be thrown off her game plan for the morning, at least she could work toward finding the human behind the robot. "You're the youngest billionaire in Savannah," she reminded him. "Heck, the entire South. Doesn't a driver come with that title?"

"That title came with a lot of hard work. Besides, I love to drive."

"So you're human?"

His locked-down tone surprised her. "More than you know."

Great. Her curiosity was growing like an overinflated balloon. Pretty soon she might explode from it—but that was better than drooling over his blond good looks.

"Why won't you share those personal reasons with me?"

She wasn't sure why she asked. Maybe to get herself away from her attraction to Royce. Maybe to dig deeper into the mysteries she had begun to see. If she hadn't been watching his face, she'd have missed the flicker of surprise that appeared on his expression before he shut back down.

"I told you, I don't want to talk about it."

He had, but that wouldn't stop her from trying. "Sometimes it helps."

"Not true."

Stubborn man. "Have you ever even tried?" She suspected not, considering that he seemed like the all-business-all-the-time type.

She could tell her question annoyed him by the way he tightened his hands on the steering wheel. "We're almost there," he said, instead of answering.

Fine.

Then Jasmine looked around, realizing exactly how far out of town they were. Uneasiness started to grow deep inside. "You realize that the farther we are from town, the less likely people are to attend the event, right?"

"Oh, they'll show up for this."

His confident tone didn't turn her into a believer—after all, she was the expert in this business.

The minute he turned down a particular driveway, her fears were confirmed. She'd only been down this driveway once. A very long time ago, and only by accident. Later when she'd started researching the place, she'd realized what it was. They could not have their event here.

"Royce, no." Her grip on the seat tightened as tension took hold of her. "We can't do this here. Do you know how long Keller House has been empty?"

"It was empty for over twenty years," he said. "The carriage house has been occupied for five years. It's currently the home of the caretaker."

Okay, so maybe she didn't know everything. "But the main house must be in need of hundreds of thousands of dollars of renovations."

"Four hundred thousand in renovations, to be exact," Royce said. She swore she could hear a smirk in his voice. "And that doesn't include the back gardens, which can't be started on until closer to spring."

She eyed him suspiciously as he pulled the car to a halt before the front steps. He looked back with perfect calm, so she turned her attention to the house. The massive gray stone building seemed sad and silent from where she sat. "And how do you know that, Royce?"

He ignored her as he exited the vehicle. She stared up at the imposing edifice, waiting for him to come around to open her door. When he did, she got out and stood in the space between the door and the car to look him straight in the eye.

"I can't oversee renovations while I'm doing an event," she said. "And what owner in the middle of renovations would want an event here?"

"No, the renovations are my job. The event is yours," he said, enunciating clearly. "Just get out of the car."

I've gone from dealing with a difficult boss to biting off more than I can chew. Jasmine stepped away from the car and stood before the mammoth building. It was gorgeous, even in its run-down state. Ivy climbed up one corner. Though cracked in a few places, the gray stone still lent a majesty to the structure. Even the steps were made of it. She could imagine women walking up them in huge hoop skirts on their way to a ball here.

"I've always been curious about this place," she said. "My sister, who is a big history buff, says that the Kellers used to be the most prominent family in Savannah. Their house was detailed in many newspaper accounts and gossip columns throughout the years. But then the entire family was wiped out by smallpox."

"Shall we go inside?" he asked.

She met his gaze. "You're serious about this?"

"I am. We will hold the masquerade here."

She glanced between him and the house that hadn't been a home to anyone in a long time. He'd gone from uninvolved to highly involved more quickly than she could wrap her brain around. "So you are a bit of a philanthropist," she said.

"No. Real estate is a good investment."

But as he turned away she glimpsed something in his expression. Something he probably didn't want her to see. She had a feeling that like the building before her, he was hiding an awful lot behind that facade of his.

Five

Just a quick walk through to see the current state of renovations, let Jasmine take a quick peek and then they'd head back to the city. That was Royce's plan, and, by damn, he was sticking to it this time.

But it wasn't helping that he found her caution amusing as she stepped through the massive antique double doors. Clearly, she expected the inside of Keller House to be a disaster.

Granted, the exterior still needed work, but there was plenty of time to get to that. The exterior would be a years-long project, just as the inside had been. And the craggy, cracked surface had character that Royce kind of enjoyed.

The wonder on her face as she took in the already renovated foyer made his heart speed up. Royce quickly looked away. *No distractions. Focus.* He had a feeling her enthusiasm, in addition to being attractive, would be infectious.

But he was here for business.

As per his usual MO, he mentally identified what he needed to do. Then he started purposefully down the main hallway that cut the house virtually in half. The kitchen lay at the other end, which was where he hoped to find his construction crew hard at work.

"Wow! Is this staircase the original? Or a reproduction?"

Royce froze. "It's the original," he conceded, then moved a few more steps. Maybe if he kept moving, she would follow.

Her gorgeous blue eyes were roving up and down the magnificent two-story structure. "It's beautiful," she breathed. "Who did the renovations?"

He took a few more steps, even though she hadn't budged. "Jasmine, I don't have much time to get this done, so if we could move on—"

She nodded and moved to follow, though her

gaze stayed glued to the refinished mahogany and blue tile patterns along the edges of the steps. He turned away and picked up speed. His brain started to produce a list of all the things he needed to discuss with the foreman.

"All these tiles...are they Italian?"

Royce heard the question but kept moving.

At first he thought he heard her following, but then the footsteps stopped and her voice sounded farther away. Royce paused, glancing over his shoulder. No Jasmine in sight. Then he realized what room she had disappeared into.

The ballroom. Of course that would interest her.

The urgent pull of business needled him to keep going. She could explore while he got things done. Problem solved. But there was also the worry that she would wander somewhere that she could get hurt. Not all the rooms were finished. Since they hadn't been expecting company, the dangerous areas weren't necessarily marked.

Then there was the question of her excitement and how he wanted to read it in her expression as she explored. He shouldn't care. The fact that he was even thinking about this meant he should keep going. Instead his steps took him back toward the open doorway.

The ballroom walls had been carefully stripped of ancient wallpaper to reveal intricate painted murals. They'd decided to clean and preserve them as is, rather than recreating them. Wear and tear showed in spots, but it was the kind of damage that one would find in an antique museum piece. It simply added to the charm. The crown molding surrounding the windows, murals and chandelier bases had been stripped and refinished in an off white. Eggshell, his mother had called it.

The elaborate crystal chandeliers had been refinished and rewired. The wood floor had been stripped of decades of dirt and grime and was waiting to be stained and protected with a thick coat of polyurethane. There was still a series of mirrors waiting to be hung.

The room was a showpiece in and of itself.

Jasmine twirled slowly in the center, taking in all the delights. She stopped as she came to face him. Some of his indecision must have come across as irritation in his expression, because her eyes widened for a moment.

Then a grin that could only be classified as cute spread across her face. "I can't help it," she said. "I need to see what I'm gonna have to work with."

"So you *do* approve?"

The expression he'd come to associate with her trying to figure out a way around him made a quick appearance. "Possibly." She turned away. The skirt of her dress swirled with her movements, giving him another glance at sculpted calves and pretty ankles. Didn't the woman ever wear pants?

"But I will need to see more before we know for sure."

Vixen. The minute the word crossed his mind, Royce had second thoughts. After all, he'd never thought about any of the other women he worked with, now or in the past, in such a way. It was surely inappropriate. But completely and totally true.

Jasmine knew exactly what she was doing—keeping him on his toes.

Resigning himself, he gestured for her to continue down the hall. "Everything else on this floor has been completed, except the kitchens." He hoped. "That's what I need to check on today."

As they made their way down the hall, he opened various doors. She got to explore. He got to maintain forward momentum. Win-win.

Only every peek into a room elicited the same excitement as a child opening presents on Christmas morning. The first gasps jumpstarted his heart, even though he tried to ignore them—and his physical reaction.

"Are these fixtures original?" she asked.

He nodded, warming to one of his favorite subjects outside of business. He and his mother had had two things in common—antiques and cooking. Their shared interests had strengthened their bond.

"All of the fixtures are original, unless they were broken beyond repair. Some of the back rooms had busted windows and weather damage, so we had to do some extensive replacements there. Everywhere else, I had what I could refinished. Some of the electrical components had to be updated. But the feel of the original should be maintained wherever possible—"

He noticed her watching him and felt a moment of unfamiliar self-consciousness. "In my opinion," he added. An opinion he had only shared with his contractor and his mother when she was still alive. Not only was it no one else's business, Royce had always found himself extremely protective of projects that he was full-on enthusiastic about.

Projects that sparked his creativity and drive, instead of the logical side of his brain. Only certain people who shared that drive were let in. He wasn't ready to let Jasmine in. These softening tendencies she inspired in him made keeping things strictly business with her an absolute must.

After what seemed like hours, they finally made it to the kitchen. Jasmine took herself off to pepper the workers with questions while Royce checked in with the foreman. He almost laughed at how short and to the point their discussion was, compared to the last hour with Jasmine. He had a feeling he would hole up in his office when he got back and communicate only by email. He'd used up his allotment of spoken words for the day.

It wasn't until they were on their way back out that Royce's relief was busted.

Jasmine's frequent glances warned him something was up. It didn't take her long to get to the point.

"One of the workers said your mother lived here."

Ah. Well, it wasn't like he'd told them to keep it a secret. "Yes. She lived in the carriage house for a few years before she died."

"I'm so sorry."

Royce just kept walking. He didn't want to get into how much he missed his mother, or how he hadn't felt he'd done everything he could for her before she died. There wasn't much point to those types of conversations.

"Was she interested in the renovations?"

Maybe they weren't done with this subject. "She definitely was. I bought the property for her, and she helped plan every facet of the renovations before she passed away. She was a history and museum buff."

"My sister loves history, too. She teaches it at

the community college. She's the one who told me about this place."

The personal nature of the conversation set off alarms in his brain, but his sudden desire to talk to someone who understood the house and his love of it overrode his caution. "We discussed everything about the direction of the renovations. How much to save. How much to gut and start over on. She loved every minute of it."

He could almost feel Jasmine's warm gaze on his face. Then she said, "I bet she did. That must have been a wonderful thing for her."

He shrugged. "It was the least I could offer her. She was a single mother my entire life. She sacrificed more than any woman should. To make her comfortable and happy was a small gift in comparison."

He remembered watching Jasmine with her daughter, and how it had given rise to the uncomfortable memories of his own childhood. He'd told the truth. His mother had sacrificed a lot. So had he. Which had fostered his attitude on single mothers and the workplace.

As they walked back down the front steps, the burning question Royce had ignored for days finally surfaced. "Jasmine, do you regret being a single mother?"

She halted abruptly. The gorgeous, expressive face he'd been surreptitiously watching all morning shut down. He should have known—should have kept his mouth shut. Reason number two that he avoided social gatherings...he wasn't great at handling casual conversation.

Then her words hit him like bullets. "Never," she said. As she turned away, she added, "Without me, she'd have no one at all."

Jasmine sprinted around the corner of her regular event photographer's house, groaning when she saw Royce sitting in his car at the curb. She'd had her sister drop her off at the side of Dominic's, hoping she wouldn't have to explain how her morning had gone. The last thing she wanted to get into was why she'd needed a ride here instead of driving herself. Of course, the fact that she was fifteen minutes late and running in her heels probably raised eyebrows.

At least she'd texted Royce and Dominic to let them know she was running behind.

She took a few seconds to straighten her dress

as Royce climbed out of his sleek car. The chaos of the morning made it a little harder to pull on her professional demeanor. She would blame that on the difficult circumstances rather than the effect every meeting with this man had on her.

Regardless, it didn't bode well for being in close proximity with Royce this morning.

Hopefully her smile wasn't strained enough to show the lack of sleep and worry. Rosie was teething again, so she hadn't slept well. Then Jasmine had worried about leaving her with Auntie when she knew her daughter would be more than a handful. And then…she'd gone out to find her car dead as a doornail.

Her frustration levels were maxed out.

She thought she'd masked her feelings pretty well, but Royce's double take as he approached her told her otherwise. For once, she prayed he'd stick to his strictly business MO. Even if she'd felt inclined to share her situation, his attitude about single mothers and the workplace gave her pause.

Instead, she tried to concentrate on the bright sunshine in hopes it would chase away her worries and gloom. Other than a brief good morning, she remained silent as they waited for Dominic to answer the bell. Unfortunately, the one day she wished Royce would stick to his robot impersonation, he had to deviate from the norm.

"Everything okay?" he asked.

This must be payback of some sort for her nosiness...

"Yes." She knew her tone would give away that she was lying.

"You seem upset."

Lord, why did she have to have such an expressive face? Why couldn't she just hide behind a stone facade? Of course, that was against her nature and normal method of dealing with clients. She liked being on friendly terms and being perceived as approachable. Which was why everything about her business interactions with Royce had felt wrong.

Fortunately Dominic opened the door of the house before she had to respond to Royce. The photographer's enthusiastic bear hug covered a lot of her strain and helped her regain her equilibrium. She'd worked with Dominic a lot over the last few years. His sheer size made clients think twice about hiring him—he looked more like a bouncer at a bar than an artist—until they saw his portfolio.

He had an ability to showcase emotion in an image that was sheer genius.

His handshake with Royce was firm but not a masculine attempt to dominate. He held the door open for them to enter the historic slate-gray and white Victorian cottage that served as his office, as well as the home that he shared with his partner, Greg.

"I'm so sorry that I was late," Jasmine said, taking a deep breath and noticing the intoxicating scent of baking cookies.

"No problem," Dominic said, always easygoing. In all the time she'd known him, she'd never seen him angry, even when dealing with some pretty demanding clients.

"Dang, Greg must be cooking," she teased. "I could gain weight just breathing." Greg was a baker who created incredible cookies and meringues in the industrial kitchen at the back of the house.

"We try," Dominic said with a wink before leading them into a nearby office. "He probably chose what to make the minute he knew you were coming over. A little sugar for our Sugar."

"He knows me well."

Just following Dominic deeper into the house helped Jasmine relax a little bit more. She'd never been the corporate office type. Her one venture into cubicle-land had convinced her it was the ninth circle of hell. Dominic's office echoed her own, though they were two totally different styles. His was comfortable, with masculine elements of leather, grommets, wrought iron. Hers was everything fluffy and feathery. But both were designed to be lived in, played in.

Which just made the work more fun.

"So, tell me a little about what you're aiming for," Dominic said, leading them to a round table in one corner.

"That would be Jasmine's department," Royce said as he held out a chair for her.

Royce might be all business, but his mama had obviously made sure he was a gentleman.

Dominic tossed Jasmine a brief glance, but she could read a wealth of questions in the look. Like, what was this guy doing here if he wasn't doing the talking? But she didn't want to get into that right now.

"We're planning a masquerade event," she said.

The light in Dominic's eyes told her he was on board already.

"But we don't want just your traditional ball," she added. "We're also looking for other options for entertainment. I was thinking about that photo booth you set up for St. Anne's."

"A photo booth?" Royce asked, the doubt clear in his tone.

"Oh, it isn't your normal photo booth," Jasmine assured him.

Dominic eagerly reached for one of the large photo albums on the table. "Check it out."

He turned the pages slowly, giving them a chance to study the various options. "We created a background unique to the event and brought in props for the guests to use." He pointed to a group of people in a rowboat in front of a mural of a lake with a decorative bridge over it.

"I was thinking a mysterious castle," Jasmine offered.

The men batted ideas around for a minute.

Against her hip, Jasmine felt her phone buzz. Since her family knew she didn't answer during meetings, she assumed it was a client and ignored it for the moment. When the buzzing started again after a few minutes, she stiffened, all her earlier tension returning.

Trying to brush it aside, she tossed out some more ideas. But the third buzz was her undoing. Slipping the phone from her pocket, she glanced at the screen. Two missed phone calls and a text from her sister Ivy.

911

She looked up to find both men watching her. Her smile was probably strained but she offered it anyway as she stood. "If you could excuse me just a moment, gentlemen?"

"Nothing wrong with that beautiful baby, I hope?" Dominic asked.

Seeing Royce's back straighten both unnerved her and ticked her off. "I certainly hope not," she said, unhappy with the quaver that had entered her voice.

But she wasn't backing down. She didn't know

what his beef was with single mothers and families, but it wasn't her problem. There was no denying she wasn't a perfect mother. She had no delusions about that. The learning curve of the last six months had been steep. Still, she'd go above and beyond for Rosie and the rest of her family.

Family was the one thing that came before her clients, regardless of what they thought.

As she stepped back out to the porch, she prayed it was something like another stalled car or a burst water pipe. Things were replaceable. People weren't. Now that Rosie was a part of their lives, she simply couldn't imagine it any other way.

"Ivy?" she asked as her youngest sister answered the phone. "What's wrong?"

"I need you quick," Ivy said, her voice trembling and breathless. "I'm at Savannah General."

Jasmine's heart thudded in her ears, cutting off Ivy's voice. The hospital? So much for her day getting easier.

Six

Royce watched Jasmine disappear out the door with her phone and was surprised at his personal concern. Ordinarily, he would have been put out. He didn't have a problem with his employees dealing with life, as long as they did it on their own time. Normally he'd be formulating a few admonishing words after she'd kept him waiting this morning and then stepped out of a business meeting to handle what was obviously a personal call.

Instead, he sat here wondering what was wrong.

He turned back to find Dominic staring at the

door with a frown on his face. The lines between his eyebrows said he was worried, too, but his expression turned more neutral when he caught Royce's look.

"Would you like to go over a few portfolios while we wait?" he asked, his voice calm even though he seemed to have other things on his mind.

Eager for a distraction, Royce gave a quick nod. Besides, they were here on business. He needed to focus.

Dominic was quick thinking and smart, which gave him a leg up in Royce's book. He pulled out examples of things he thought might work from the limited knowledge he had of their plans. Royce was impressed. He kept looking through one of the books while they discussed some photo booth ideas. Still, the whole time, his brain was ticking off the minutes that Jasmine had been gone.

What was going on? Did she need help?

As if his very thoughts had conjured her up, Royce turned the page to see a grouping of photos featuring Jasmine and her daughter. There was also another woman in the outdoor portraits, which seemed to have been taken at one of the local squares. The fountain behind them was familiar. The greenery provided a lush frame for the women.

"Oh, I'd forgotten which book those were in," Dominic said, surveying the spread with a smile.

Despite admonishing himself to focus on the meeting, Royce found himself tilting the album farther toward him so he could study the group of women more closely. Jasmine was her usual elegant self, her summer dress full and flowing with a fitted bodice. This was his first time seeing her hair down around her shoulders. The thick mass blanketed her pale skin in soft waves, the sunshine creating glossy highlights in the dark color.

Rosie looked to be newborn, but there was no mistaking those black curls. The other woman looked down at the baby with a smile. But upon closer inspection, Royce thought he detected a pervasive sadness in the woman's gaze that belied her indulgent expression as she watched the child.

Royce detected another subtle difference among the three. The third woman seemed sick.

Her skin appeared a little gray, a little more aged than Jasmine's.

Though the three were grouped close together on a picnic blanket in dappled sunshine beneath the trees, the other woman seemed to be more of an observer than part of the group. Still, Dominic was definitely talented when it came to composing a shot.

"The resemblance is remarkable," Royce murmured. All that dark hair linked the women together. No male could penetrate their bond. Only it made him curious about Rosie's father and whether she looked like him at all…

No. He refused to entertain any thoughts like that. It was too personal…too tempting…

"I know," Dominic was saying. "Hard to believe they aren't even related, isn't it? You'd never know Jasmine wasn't Rosie's biological mother."

Royce's gaze snapped up to the other man. "What?"

Dominic's eyes widened. "Well…"

Without me, she'd have no one at all. Jasmine's words came back to him, haunting his mind.

"What do you mean, Dominic?" Royce forced

himself to keep his voice nonchalant. He kept all urgency out of the question. Even though, suddenly, he wanted to know very, very badly.

"I'm not sure I should share Jasmine's personal business," Dominic said with a frown. "I spoke out of turn."

"I understand. I just wondered because Jasmine seemed so natural with her daughter. I knew she was a single mother," he added, sprinkling in the truth, "but I never would have guessed she hadn't given birth to her."

Dominic seemed to consider his words. "You've seen her with Rosie?"

"Sure. She brought her to the office the other day." Royce wasn't going to reveal any more details about that visit...details that would make him look bad.

"Oh, yeah. Rosie's such a good baby. Jasmine can pretty much take her wherever and the little one is perfectly content. And will charm anyone within smiling distance."

Which just resurrected images of the sleepy child grinning in Jasmine's arms. They'd looked so perfect together, which made it hard to believe that Jasmine wasn't the birth mother.

Royce tried to assimilate the new things he'd learned into the old image, but it wasn't working very well. An odd feeling started in his chest. And feelings weren't a normal occurrence when he conducted business. Yet he seemed to be having them more and more often around Jasmine Harden.

He needed to get a hold on that…later.

"Is this Rosie's mom?" he asked without thinking.

Dominic paused again, then shrugged. "Yeah. Jasmine met her at City Sanctuary mission. I'm not sure about the details, but I know Jasmine's family took her in early in her pregnancy. Something went wrong and she asked Jasmine to take Rosie if anything happened." He looked down at the smiling women in the picture. "She never even hesitated."

Royce wasn't surprised. Jasmine was strong. She ran a successful business and had a great reputation. He imagined she'd tackled motherhood with the same determination and grace.

He should be ashamed of thinking any differently. Except now he wanted the whole story.

"Dominic, will you call me a cab, please?" Jasmine's voice quavered as she asked the question.

Royce hadn't even realized Jasmine had reentered the office. He glanced up. Her expression was calm, but Royce could see the strain around her delicate mouth and eyes.

Dominic stood. "Sugar, what's wrong?"

Jasmine visibly pulled herself together. "I'm so sorry to cut this short, but Auntie is at the hospital. She fell."

As Dominic made the appropriate remarks, Royce stood. This type of thing was totally out of his realm of expertise.

He watched as Dominic slid an arm around Jasmine's shoulders, feeling completely lost in this situation. That's when he realized he didn't need to do that part. Dominic had taken care of the comfort side of things. Royce could go straight to the logistics of the situation—which was his area of expertise.

"Where's your car?" he asked, his tone now brooking no arguments.

She wouldn't look him straight in the eye, but mumbled, "It wouldn't start this morning. My sister Willow brought me."

No wonder she'd looked frazzled when she arrived.

"Let me cancel my next few appointments and we'll head over," Dominic said.

"Absolutely not," she countered, although her eyes were starting to look suspiciously glassy. "Just call me a cab."

As they argued with each other, Royce argued with himself. So she had no car. She needed to go to the hospital. A cab would take forever.

He didn't want to get involved in her personal life.

But she didn't have a car.

And he was an ass for even debating this with himself. Finally, he cut them both off with, "It looks like I'm your ride."

For the second time that day, Jasmine found herself riding in Royce's car. Sitting next to him reminded her of all the reasons she shouldn't be here.

The subtly spicy smell of him. The sight of his sure hands on the wheel. The overt luxury of the vehicle.

It was too intimate. Too much. There were too

many reasons she should stay far away from personal situations with Mr. Business.

But what choice did she have?

Taking Dominic away from his other clients didn't seem fair, though he'd been more than willing to help her out as a friend. A cab would have taken a while. She needed to get to Auntie and Rosie as soon as possible. It was her job to take care of her fam—

"Who is Auntie?"

It took Jasmine a moment to register Royce's words because she'd completely blocked out any chance of his asking her a question about herself. Their few personal interactions so far had seemed as awkward for him as they had been for her. Maybe she'd been wrong.

"She's not really my aunt," Jasmine clarified. "She was my mother's nanny when she was little and my grandmother's best friend. We moved in with her after...anyway, all of us girls still live together now."

Royce nodded. She could see the movement out of the corner of her eye, even though she refused to look directly at him. His presence was overpowering in the small space, especially in her vulnerable state. It was simply too close for comfort.

"She must be older," Royce surmised. "A fall can be pretty serious in those circumstances."

Which was a fact Jasmine wasn't ready to confront. They'd be at the hospital soon enough, and she'd deal with it then. "She helps with Rosie when none of us girls are able to be home."

"I know one of your sisters is a college professor. What does the other one do?"

"She's an executive assistant at the McLemore firm."

"That's good. I'm glad you all are close and you have that kind of support. Rosie won't be alone when her mom's working."

Jasmine felt her body stiffen in defense, but something about the sad tone of his voice had her reconsidering. Before she could question it, he went on.

"Why didn't you tell me Rosie was adopted?"

The world swirled around Jasmine for a moment, disorienting her. This whole line of questioning was completely out of character for Royce. "I didn't realize you would care."

Why would he? Every encounter with her

daughter, or even talking about her, seemed to bring a negative reaction from him.

As if he didn't realize the intent behind her answer, he mused, "You look so much alike. It never occurred to me."

Jasmine was getting more confused by the minute, but at least it kept her worry about Auntie at bay. It also loosened the hold she normally kept on her tongue in front of her clients. "I truly don't understand, Royce. What difference does it make? I'm her mother. I'm a damn good one. I would never deny her a home or neglect her to go out to earn a living."

"Why wouldn't you?"

The car came to an abrupt halt. At first, Jasmine thought she'd pushed too far. Then she realized he'd actually parked in a parking space. They'd arrived at the hospital more quickly than she'd expected.

Only as he was climbing out of the door did he answer. "My mom did."

As he softly shut the door, then walked around the car, Jasmine sat in stunned silence. Not only because Royce had admitted something so personal, but because it contradicted everything he'd told her about his mother at Keller House. He opened the door and helped her out as if he hadn't just dropped a bombshell of magnificent proportions on her. They walked into the hospital in silence.

What should she say?

He'd taken care of his mother before she died. She'd lived in the carriage house for years. Her son was Savannah's youngest, and most mysterious, billionaire. Had whatever happened to his mother colored how he saw women, how he saw Jasmine?

His earlier comment made the answer obvious.

Before she could get a handle on her reaction, they reached the waiting area where Ivy was sitting with Rosie. Thankfully, the baby was sleeping, though her pudgy cheeks were flushed with the slight fever Jasmine was learning to associate with her teething spells.

Jasmine leaned over to carefully hug her sister around the sleeping child. "What did the doctors say?" she asked as she crouched in front of the pair.

"We're still waiting on the X-rays to find out." Ivy worried her lower lip, making her look a lot older than her twenty-three years. "I'm sorry you had to come here. I just didn't know what to do."

"No. It's fine," Jasmine said. Though asking Ivy not to feel bad was like asking Jasmine not to worry. "The last thing I would have wanted was for you to be sitting here by yourself dealing with all of this. It's no problem at all."

"But your car—"

"Driving over here wasn't a big deal," Royce interjected. "We were about done, anyway."

Ivy glanced at him, her eyes growing wide with surprise.

"You had to get him to drive you?" she breathed. "I'm so sorry."

"Car trouble always hits at the worst possible moment." Royce tried to reassured her.

It didn't work too well. Jasmine spied a slight sheen of tears in her sister's eyes before she dropped her gaze and placed a kiss on Rosie's head. It still amazed her that her littlest sister handled difficult clients with such ease at work. Jasmine still saw her as the child in need of her protection and care. But in this situation, they were going to support each other through whatever challenges they faced.

"Is everybody okay?" Willow rushed up behind them.

Ivy stood as they all talked over each other, trying to share what they knew and offer comfort. Though Jasmine still felt a touch of panic over Auntie's condition, it was better with both of her sisters here. Out of the corner of her eye, she spied Royce standing to the side, watching them. His expression was carefully neutral. With a quick squeeze of her sisters' arms, she walked over to where he stood.

"Thank you so much for bringing me here. I didn't intend to disrupt your day."

A slight frown snuck across his face, but wasn't there long enough for Jasmine to figure out what it meant. Ivy appeared at her elbow with a blinking Rosie. Jasmine smiled at the little girl and got a crooked grin in return. Taking her into her arms, Jasmine hugged her close for a moment. Then she turned her focus back to Royce. She definitely noticed how his gaze had settled directly on her, avoiding Rosie completely.

Without thought, she softly asked, "Why would your mother leave you alone?"

For a brief second, she saw a flash of pain in

his expression that was so intense it took Jasmine back to the days and weeks right after her parents had been killed in the car accident. But within the space of a blink, the emotion disappeared. Had she imagined it? When he dropped his gaze to Rosie, it made her wonder.

Then a nurse called from behind him, "King family?"

Recognizing Auntie's last name, she handed Rosie over to Willow and rushed to the edge of the waiting area. But the nurse wasn't very helpful, and Jasmine found herself returning with a clipboard in her hand.

"What did she say?" Willow demanded.

Jasmine shook her head, blinking so tears wouldn't well up in her eyes. "Just that they were waiting to take her to X-ray, and in the meantime they needed this paperwork filled out."

Seven

Royce shifted uncomfortably as he watched Jasmine blink before looking at her sisters. He remembered the many brave faces he'd put on with no one there to take notice except his mother. Turning away from the reminder, he took a seat across from Jasmine's sisters in the waiting room.

Jasmine settled into a chair and started on the paperwork. Her sisters studied him with varying degrees of interest.

"Is there a problem, ladies?" he finally asked.

"Why didn't Jasmine take a cab?" Willow asked.

"It would have taken too long."

"One of us could have picked her up," Willow said.

This felt a little like a what-are-your-intentions interrogation, not that he had any experience with those. Or with anything in this situation, really. Long-fallow instincts had kicked in when he'd seen Jasmine in need, overriding his usual laser focus on business.

"That would have taken even longer," he said, attempting to soften his clipped tone since they were just trying to look out for their sister. "Besides, my mother wouldn't have appreciated me leaving a lady high and dry."

The two women shared a look, one that should have made him very suspicious. But, like all good businessmen, Royce held his tongue. He knew better than to give them extra ammunition, especially when he wasn't sure what the bullet was actually made of in this instance.

Suddenly both women glanced down. Following their gaze, he took in how Rosie was snuggled up against Ivy. Her eyelids drooped. He could see the softening effect the little cutie had on Ivy and Willow, and even felt an echo deep inside himself. He hadn't dealt with so many emotions since his mother died.

Was it being in this place? The same hospital where they'd spent her last days? Or was it these women? Seeing their interactions, how they cared for each other, he found it fascinating. A little scary, too. Being the focus of their attention wasn't comfortable at all.

Like his mother, they seemed to be able to see past the front he presented to the world to the actual man beneath. He could almost feel the crack in his protective wall. He wasn't very comfortable with that.

Yet he couldn't bring himself to leave.

He reached out one hand to rub it gently against Rosie's chubby, flushed cheek. "She feels a little feverish."

"She's been teething," Ivy explained. "Which means she's often fussy and not sleeping well, poor thing."

"Poor Mama," Willow added, giving the little girl a loving look. "I don't think Jasmine's had a full night's sleep in days."

Which explained why Rosie was so tired today. But Royce knew absolutely nothing about babies and teething, so he switched subjects. Anything to distract himself from the memories whirling through his mind. "So, what do you ladies do for a living?" he asked, even though Jasmine had already told him the answer.

Willow jumped in easily. "I teach history at the community college."

Royce nodded. "Any specialties?"

"American and local history. When you're descended from a pirate family, you can't help but immerse yourself in Savannah's colorful past."

"I'd imagine." Somehow he wasn't surprised to find Jasmine had some pirate blood in her. She certainly drove a hard bargain to get exactly what she wanted.

Ivy filled the pause. "I'm the executive assistant to Paxton McLemore."

That was interesting. "Intense guy to work for, isn't he?"

"At times, but I love it. Challenging but enjoyable."

Obviously they were a family of very smart women who were very good at standing on their own two feet, making their way in the world after losing their parents. He could relate. Impressive.

But, unlike him, they weren't focused only on making money. He thought over all the charitable causes for which Jasmine had coordinated events. The dossier his assistant had put together had been more than impressive.

As she rose and crossed the room to return the clipboard to a woman behind the desk, he couldn't help but think of all she'd dealt with at home while she'd been pulling off those events. Unlike Royce, she didn't go home, put up her feet and catch up on her rest after a hard day's work.

No, she worked just as hard at home. If not harder. She kept her family together and fed. Took on the role of mother. And apparently offered hands-on help to the charity she'd chosen to support with his event.

Her life had turned out very differently from his.

The women across from him went suddenly silent. Royce followed their gaze to see Jasmine slowly approach from across the room. Before he knew it, her sisters were on their feet.

Royce watched the baby pass from sister to sister with a kind of bewilderment and an incredible calm. Until inevitably the baby was passed to him, and he found himself standing alone in the waiting room with the child snuggled carefully in the crook of his arm. He watched as the girls disappeared around a column and joined their sister.

He glanced down at the baby now in his arms. She was so small. Yet when she was awake and her eyes were open, that small body came alive with personality. Even at her young age.

As Jasmine turned back toward the hall, the child gave a shuddering breath, evoking sympathy for how miserable she must be at the moment. She probably wished she was home in her own bed instead of being carried around a noisy hospital waiting room.

Though he knew she couldn't have heard it from where she stood, Jasmine froze. Then she whipped her head around to survey her sisters. "Where's Rosie?"

As if passing the buck, both women pointed in his direction. Jasmine's eyes went wide with shock. But as she glanced down to see Rosie still sleeping, the tears that she'd held back earlier finally overflowed.

As the women before him sniffled and hugged each other, Royce moved closer to stand outside their circle with the baby nestled in his arms. For a brief moment, something akin to panic welled up in Royce's chest. A feeling he hadn't experienced since he'd first realized he was completely alone in the world. As if these people he barely knew had abandoned him.

Crazy.

A noise caught his attention. He glanced down, meeting wide dark eyes. The one difference between Rosie and Jasmine. The baby's eyes were dark and oddly wise. But beautiful. Compelling. Royce found himself as mesmerized as he'd been by his first glimpse of her mother's bright blue eyes.

Suddenly he realized that he was bouncing the baby slightly. It was a rhythm entirely seated in his bones, natural but unfamiliar. And he couldn't stop.

"King?" a nurse called from across the room. "The King family?" He looked up.

The women before him seemed completely oblivious. Stepping closer, he adopted a firm, no-nonsense tone. "Ladies, let's go see what the nurse has to say."

Immediately their tears stopped and they started across the room. "Purses," he reminded them.

They paused to rapidly scoop up all their stuff, then he ushered them across the carpeted floor to the staff member. She smiled, as if she were completely used to such a delay. He'd watched enough waiting room drama when his mother was sick to know she probably was.

Jasmine shifted impatiently as the nurse waited for all the sisters to gather around her. Then she said, "I wanted to assure you it's just a sprain..." She glanced around, meeting everyone's gaze. "It's a bad one, though. The doctor can explain more, if one of you would like to come back and speak with him."

"You, Jasmine," Willow said. "You'll remember more of the details than I will."

The nurse nodded, but Royce stepped forward. He kept his voice low, but firm. "Is there any possibility we could all go back with you? I realize the rooms are small, but the little one isn't going to do well without her mother."

The nurse took one look at Rosie and Royce could see her refusal melt on her tongue. "Poor baby. Is it a fever?"

"Just a low-grade one," Jasmine rushed in to answer. "From teething. She isn't sick."

"Oh, but that makes babies miserable, doesn't it?" The nurse cooed at Rosie for a few moments, gaining a gummy grin; Royce spotted just a hint of a tooth breaking the front skin. "Of course you need to be with your mama." Some semblance of a stern look returned to the nurse's face, but it lacked conviction. "But if it gets full in there, you'll have to wait across the hall."

"Not a problem," Royce said, eager to go now that he'd gotten his way.

The last thing he wanted was to split up the three women or find himself alone with the baby in his arms, which seemed to be drawing out all kinds of emotions he didn't want to handle.

Rosie was really good while they met with the doctor and received his instructions. After all of his experiences with his own mother, Royce knew that physical therapy wouldn't be easy for

Auntie, but would be worth it for her to get fully back on her feet at her advanced age.

The half-jiggling, half-bouncing motion Royce's body had adopted worked wonders, but before long a little whimper erupted. A streak of panic burned through Royce, but he refused to let it show.

It almost slipped through when he found the women watching him. Royce had an uncomfortable feeling they were finally evaluating his child-holding skills and finding him lacking.

"What?" he asked in a soft tone.

"Aren't you the guy Jasmine said didn't care about anything but business?" Ivy's blue eyes dropped to the baby in his arms.

He wasn't offended. "I'd say that would be an accurate description." Did he owe them an explanation? Did he even have one for why he was here right this moment?

As they stood around the tiny cubicle where Auntie lay in the hospital bed, Willow dug into the diaper bag she held. "Here," she said, holding out a ring-shaped toy. "Let's try this. Want me to take her?"

Royce took the toy but shook his head. "Actually, I want you to go get your car and pull it around to the entrance."

Willow glanced around. "But they haven't discharged Auntie yet."

"I'll help your sisters take care of that," Royce assured her. "You just bring the car around."

Willow nodded uncertainly, then kissed Auntie and went for the car.

Jasmine watched her go. "Why is she getting the car so early?"

"Because we're leaving," Royce assured her. "I want you to get Auntie dressed."

When she opened her mouth to question him, Royce simply shook his head. "Just do it."

Turning away, he went to find the nurse at her station. She watched him struggle with the now squirming baby; her teething ring was no longer keeping her occupied. "I know you have a lot going on around here," he said, "but we need to get this one home before we have a full-blown scene."

His only knowledge of babies was of them crying in restaurants and stores. He had no idea what would set Rosie off, but he'd use her to their advantage in getting Auntie released sooner.

The nurse cooed at Rosie, nodding her head. So at least he was right in one sense.

"I have my hands full with the ladies...all the ladies," he said with a smile. "Could you possibly help us out and get Ms. King released before things go downhill?"

Seeing the nurse snap into action, Royce had to wonder how much more he could accomplish in life if he had a baby as his wingman.

Less than twenty minutes later they were headed for the car. It was unprecedented in Royce's experience with hospitals, but he wasn't going to look a gift horse in the mouth. Willow was right up front, waiting for them.

The nurse who had wheeled Ms. King out got her settled into the front passenger seat with minimal effort while Jasmine supervised. Then Jasmine turned to look at him. She shook her head. "I can't believe you managed that." A gorgeous touch of pink lit up her pale cheeks. "And managed Rosie. That was incredible."

"Only to be thwarted by something as simple as a child's car seat," he replied as he nodded toward the contraption in the back seat.

Jasmine's eyes widened and she smiled. "Right. These things look way more complicated than they are. After all you've done, though, I think we'll overlook your shortcomings on that score," she said, taking the baby from him.

There was the sassy woman he'd come to know.

In two minutes, she had Rosie deftly strapped in and content with her pacifier. Closing the door, Jasmine again gifted him with a smile. Maybe he was tired after the morning drama. Maybe he was still feeling the effects from holding the tiny, innocent child in his arms. Whatever it was, this smile snuck through his usual defenses and hit his heart with unerring accuracy.

"I still don't know how you managed it," Jasmine said. "I was so focused on Auntie and my sisters and taking care of them. But we are very, very grateful."

And that's when he stupidly ran off at the

mouth before thinking. "I'm glad to know all of my experience came in handy. My mother had a very long stay at this hospital before she died here."

Eight

Jasmine sucked in a deep breath as she saw Royce slip through the coffee shop door. Her stomach churned, forcing her to leave her café au lait untouched. She had no idea how to act after their last encounter.

No idea how to return to business as usual.

The week he had been out of town since Auntie's fall should have helped give her some perspective. Frankly, it hadn't. Because her thoughts of Royce had turned very personal and she had no idea how to combat that. Except to only talk about business.

She could do that, right?

But his smile as he sat down wasn't business as usual. It sped her heart up a little...okay, more than a little. This wasn't right.

She glared at the green ring sparkling in the sunlight for a moment.

"Everything okay?" Royce asked as he sat down with his coffee.

"Sure," Jasmine said, consciously forcing herself to relax. "I appreciate you coming."

Reaching down, she pulled several small poster boards from her bag. "I've put together some visuals for you to see what the decorator is suggesting."

"I'm amazed you're only letting me view pictures, rather than insisting I attend an actual meeting with her."

Jasmine froze for a moment. Was he complaining because she'd excluded him? "Well, with you out of town, then her going out of town, I just thought this might be easier."

To her shock, his hand lightly covered one of hers. "It's okay, Jasmine. I'm just teasing you."

"Teasing me?" She almost swallowed her tongue, because teasing had never been on Royce's agenda.

"Yes," he said, drawing the word out. "After all, you've stuck to your stipulation that I attend every planning meeting pretty hard. I can't believe you're letting me slide on this one..."

Feeling like she'd stepped into an alternate reality, one that tempted her with the idea that Royce might actually be human after all, she grinned. "Well, everyone should get time off for good behavior."

His laugh rang out, startling her. The sound was oh, so sexy. Over his shoulder, she saw several patrons glance their way, most grinning in response to his amusement. Only one didn't seem amused, a rather dour, expensively dressed man at a choice table by the window overlooking the river.

Jasmine would rather focus on the man opening up right in front of her.

She pointed out the various options depicted in the photographs. The dark purple-and-black color scheme was her favorite, with highlights of white and bright red. The elaborate table schemes included taper candles and crystals to mimic the chandeliers. Lots of rich fabric and sparkling highlights.

Event planning was her passion, so she could have gone on forever, but noticed the minute Royce's gaze started to glaze over. "Okay," she conceded, "I think I've tortured you enough."

"Honestly, give me the details of a ship's engine any day as opposed to decorating details. I only agreed to meet in the coffee shop so I'd have this to keep me awake." He lifted his coffee a few inches off the table. But it was the sheepish grin that got to her.

She'd never imagined seeing that expression on this driven businessman's face. Unfortunately, she liked it. Too much.

"So how are Ms. King and Rosie?"

"Oh, she'd just want you to call her Auntie."

He nodded, his expression remaining open in a way she wasn't quite used to or comfortable with.

"Physical therapy is going well, although she hates it."

Royce shrugged. "Who wouldn't? It's torture."

"Even more so for her, because she thinks it's a burden to everyone that we're juggling her appointments with our jobs and Rosie's care. As if that matters to any of us girls."

"My mother was like that," Royce said, staring down into his cup. "She didn't ever want to tell me when she had a doctor's appointment or treatment—she felt it took me away from more important things."

When he looked up, his eyes were serious in the same way she'd seen at the hospital. "But she got over it after the one time she took a cab to the hospital for a chemo treatment. After that, she knew in no uncertain terms I would be there for every appointment, no matter what I had going on."

That had to have been a huge concession for such a driven man.

This led her to say what had been on her mind for over a week. "I really do appreciate all you did for us, for me, at the hospital. Especially knowing that there had to be a lot of bad memories associated with that place."

"It was nothing—"

"Don't."

When he finally looked at her, she reached out and cupped his hand where it lay on the table. "It wasn't nothing. No man in that frame of mind should have to hold a teething six-month-old for that long—it was a tremendous help to us. I won't let you dismiss that."

He glanced down at her hand over his. It wasn't until several moments later—moments of anticipation that caused Jasmine to shake inside—that he spoke.

"My mother, no matter how sick she was, always had a kind word for everyone she came across at that hospital. She would help in any way she could, sometimes even pushing herself past what she was capable of to help her fellow patients."

"And you were there to help her?"

"As much as possible." Still he wouldn't look up at her.

She couldn't resist pushing a little farther. "But I don't understand. You say she took care of you, you took care of her, but also that she abandoned you. What happened?"

"It wasn't because she didn't want me…" His husky voice trailed off. Beneath her palm, she felt his hand curl into a fist. Then she noticed the shadow across their table.

Glancing up, she found the stern man from the far table standing over them. He didn't look her way or acknowledge her. His gaze was trained tightly on Royce as he said in a gruff voice, "Getting involved with your employees never leads to anything good."

Then he turned and walked away.

"That was my father. Guess he didn't want to stick around and be introduced."

The bitterness in his own voice made Royce cringe.

Jasmine glanced over her shoulder to watch the man disappear out the door. "I'm confused," she murmured.

Join the club.

"He looked familiar," she said with a faraway tone in her voice.

Though he never talked about him, just this once Royce was happy to provide the basics. "He should. His name is John Nave."

He could see the light of recognition dawning in her sexy blue eyes. "That's right. *The* John Nave, from one of the oldest families in Savannah, and one of the richest."

"But I don't understand..." Jasmine said,

her brow wrinkling in confusion. "He's your father?"

"My mother was his housekeeper." Royce hated saying it that way, because it sounded like he was defining his mother by her profession when she'd been so much more.

To her credit, Jasmine's expression didn't change. If anything, it turned a little stiff. "I'll be honest, I'm appalled he would say something like that to you, considering..."

She didn't know the half of it. "That's mild, for him. When he bothers to acknowledge me at all, he's usually pretty nasty."

"But isn't he married?"

"To one of the coldest women in the world," he murmured. "But that was a while after my mother had broken contact with him."

"How did your mother manage?" Jasmine whispered, her voice full of empathy.

"When she didn't get rid of me like he wanted, it took her a long time to find more work. But when she did, she worked her fingers to the bone, because the bastard made sure she couldn't get a judge in the county to award her child support."

Jasmine closed her eyes tightly, shaking her

head. When she opened them, he noticed the glossy sheen of tears.

Were they for him? No one but his mother had ever shed a tear over the way he'd been treated.

"I'd like to say it surprises me," Jasmine said, "but I've seen it often enough at the mission. Dads who simply couldn't care less about a child out in the world with their DNA. Men who would have preferred for them to die than take on any obligation in their own lives."

Oh, how well he knew that type.

She leaned back, studying him. He wasn't sure when she'd stopped touching his hand, but he felt the loss of contact keenly. "I'm not really upset about me," he said, waving the thought away as if it were a particle of dust in the air. "It's more about my mom. What she was left to deal with."

"That's why she left you, isn't it?"

He glanced over her shoulder instead of looking into her eyes and seeing the knowledge there. He nodded. "She had to work a lot to keep us afloat."

"And you made it up to her."

Royce sat a little straighter. "I did. She loved that house. She used to work there when she first started." He could remember long stories she would tell about the few parties she'd helped serve at, then caring for the house until it was closed. "I wanted her to be in a place she loved, so I bought it for her."

Jasmine covered his hand with hers once more. "That's wonderful, Royce."

"It's what she deserved after all of her sacrifices for me. By damn, I was going to give it to her." He let a little smile slip out. "She was happy."

"She never fell in love again?" Jasmine asked. "Never wanted to have more children?"

"When would she have had the time? Nope. She loved me, but she wanted no more children to complicate her life. And I'll never have children, either."

Jasmine didn't draw up in shocked outrage the way he might have expected. She simply asked, "Why not?"

"I've made my choice. Business is a demanding mistress. I refuse to do both."

She pressed her lips together for a moment before letting herself speak. "It's a shame. You were good with Rosie."

"Raising a child is a lot different than holding one for thirty minutes."

She smiled, though there was a hint of sadness around the edges. "I'm learning that all too well. My mother died, too, when I was fifteen."

He'd gotten that impression but never asked the details.

"Both of my parents, actually. They were killed in an automobile accident." She absently ran her finger around the edge of her cup. "We came to live with Auntie. She took all three of us in when we had no other place to go. No other relatives. Not even distant ones."

"That's a big responsibility."

"Auntie said something to me then. Something I've never forgotten, even though I didn't fully embrace it at the time."

"What's that?"

"That children aren't everyone's cup of tea."

It made sense, especially to Royce.

Jasmine wasn't done, though. That sad smile returned as she added, "But some people should learn to be tea drinkers."

Nine

"I really don't see why we need to do this," Royce said as Jasmine approached over the cracked and broken sidewalk. "It's not necessary."

And here she thought she'd loosened him up a little. Especially after the surprisingly personal meeting at the coffee shop a few days ago. Of course, the way he'd conceded the design choices with a curt "You know better than I" should have reminded her he didn't want a say in everything.

"It's not necessary to educate yourself about the charity you are promoting with your big-ticket event?"

"I told you the charity was your choice."

She could just get right to the point, but why not enjoy teasing him for a minute? "What's the big deal? So you spend a few hours down here on a Saturday. What else are you gonna do? Work?"

They shared a look, his blue eyes narrowing as if he was contemplating retribution for her sarcasm.

"Just consider this part of your job," she said. "Trust me, I've been to dozens of these charity events. You're gonna get asked lots of questions about City Sanctuary mission. Do you want to appear ignorant?"

"I could refer them to you."

"And still appear ignorant. Especially to the Jeffersons."

He grimaced, probably because he knew she was right. "It should be enough that I'm donating money."

"Don't sulk, Scrooge. You just might enjoy yourself."

His eyes widened just a notch at her tone, but she ignored it and headed for the entrance. The parking area was hidden from view of the building by a tall retaining wall that supported the elevated ground the original church had been built upon. Excitement filled her as they made their way to the break in the wall for the stairs leading to the lawn. There she caught the first glimpse of the ancient stone chapel. Though the additions made to the compound over the years didn't entirely match the architecture of the original building, which had stood since just a few decades after Savannah was founded, they didn't detract from the atmosphere, either.

Jasmine followed the gravel path with ease, having developed a familiarity with the place after years of volunteering here. She greeted the regulars as they passed.

She'd always felt safe here. The mission's destitute clients had never scared her. She'd experienced more fear among Savannah's elite, to be honest.

Everyone she greeted along the way to the entrance followed the same pattern: a smile and hello for her, then a quick suspicious glance at the man behind her. Strangers to the mission were often regarded that way, at first, but this was probably enhanced because she'd never been here with a man. Usually she was alone; only occasionally did she visit with her sisters.

They entered through the main registration lobby, where Jasmine paused. "This is the area where most public traffic comes in," she said. "Overnight guests are assigned their spaces, and those who need other services are directed to the areas or personnel they need."

She waved to the couple who usually handled the front lobby on Saturdays, then led Royce to the first large hallway. "The building was originally a church, and has been added to over the years. This makes it a little confusing for newcomers." She gestured to the left. "There are offices down here. A couple of classrooms where we hold seminars or tutoring. And there's a closet at the far end where we store used clothing to hand out."

After giving him a minute to process, she turned right. "The main dining area is at the back. I'll take you there in a little while. It was the most recent area to be updated, because part of it collapsed during the last hurricane that came through. A tree fell on it, so we had to do some structural repairs."

They stepped through a set of double doors into a gymnasium with a scuffed but decent floor. Royce, who had been silent the whole time, took in the group of children playing basketball. "This looks nice."

"It is—we use it for some after-school programs and there's actually a men's basketball group that meets here. Anyone in the building is allowed to participate." She nodded toward the far corner. "But here's the problem. This room has to serve double duty."

"Are those beds?"

"Foldaway cots. We have a women's dorm in the back, which has a leaking roof. The old chapel serves to shelter small family units when necessary. This is the men's dorm. So every night we have to pull the beds out onto the floor and every morning they are stripped and put away."

"That's a lot of work," he murmured.

"It is." She took a deep breath, almost afraid to share her hopes for the fund-raising event. "The neighbors here were an elderly couple and they gifted their land to the mission upon their deaths. But there aren't any funds to build on it." She met his solemn gaze. "A fully functioning building with single-purpose sleeping quarters would make a big difference in this part of Savannah."

"Miss Harden! Watch this!"

Jasmine glanced over as one of her little tagalongs, Oliver, jumped toward the basketball net. At five, he wasn't tall enough to make headway, but he had enough enthusiasm to make his jump impressive. "Great job!" she yelled back.

He dribbled the ball over to them, showing off his skills. "Look what I learned to do." He grabbed the ball up and rolled it across his outstretched arms and along the back of his neck.

Jasmine laughed. "Well, that's pretty cool. But how is it gonna help you play basketball?"

"Mr. Mike said it will help me learn dex—um, dexter—"

"Dexterity?" Royce offered.

"That was it."

"I see," Jasmine said. "You are well on your way to being a professional ball player, in my opinion."

The little boy stopped moving and gave her a cheeky grin. "Didn't you say you don't know anything about basketball?"

She brushed her knuckles against his cheek. "That's true. But I know determination when I see it, and you have tons of that, my sweet."

He giggled, then dribbled the ball back toward the court. She smiled after him. "He's such a cutie. His mama named him Oliver after a cocky, sneaky cat in a cartoon. I have a feeling he's gonna live up to the name."

Instead of a chuckle, Royce said, "My mother named me after my father's car."

She swiveled to face him. "What?"

"My father's Rolls Royce. He told her the only thing he'd ever loved was his car. Guess it was some kind of dig to remind him that a kid deserved love, too. Didn't work so well."

"Or maybe it was to remind her that she got the better end of that deal."

"What do you mean?"

"Cars don't give an awful lot of love in return, Royce."

As they turned back toward the main building, Jasmine spouted facts about the various aspects of the homeless mission's programs. Royce wasn't tracking. Her words from the gym kept

ringing in his ears. He couldn't help but wonder—were they true?

"Jasmine, *ma fleur*. So wonderful to see you."

Royce forced himself to tune in as they were
approached by a man in khaki pants and a polo
shirt. Jasmine introduced him as Francis Staten,
the director of the mission.

"So wonderful to meet you," Francis said with
a firm handshake that matched his calm, com-
petent expression. "We are so grateful for what
you are doing for us."

Royce was having none of that. "You know
I can't take the credit. Jasmine is the one who
brought the need to my attention."

Francis smiled. "And *you* must know that with
her running your event, it will be very successful."

"That's my sincere belief, also," Royce agreed.

Francis gave an appreciative chuckle. "Before
she combusts from that blush, shall I show you
around?"

Jasmine smiled in a sheepish way. "Well,
we've already looked over the gym, front offices and lobby."

"Excitement got the better of you, huh?" Francis asked as they headed farther down the hallway toward the back of the building. "I've never had a more enthusiastic volunteer than Jasmine here. She was such a sad girl when she first came to us, and she has become the mission's biggest asset."

"All of our volunteers are," Jasmine insisted.

That blush sure was cute.

As they crossed through a large double doorway into a spacious banquet room, Francis explained, "This is our main dining area, with industrial kitchens on the other side of those serving tables. The kitchens were refurbished by a major pledge drive. We serve hundreds of meals per day. The kitchen updates made it so much easier to keep the food fresh, hot and plentiful."

The long room was broken up by rows of tables and chairs. Only about a third of them were occupied at this time on a Saturday. "We'll start serving lunch soon," Francis said.

A lady sitting at the first table with a group of her friends called out to Jasmine and waved. With a smile, Jasmine excused herself to go over to them. Royce and Francis watched as she hugged each woman in the small group.

"She's incredible," Francis said. "A young woman who lives her beliefs, rather than simply talking about them."

He glanced over at Royce, lowering his voice a touch. "Have you met Rosie?"

Royce nodded. His stomach flipped as he imagined Rosie in this environment. Her birth mother had been a frequent guest here, so Rosie would have grown up with no stable, secure home base. "She's a beautiful little girl," he murmured. "It's hard to tell she was adopted."

"Indeed," Francis agreed. "Jasmine had known Rosie's mother for several years. One thing you learn very quickly here—you can't force your own beliefs or preferences on those who aren't as fortunate. You can only offer them whatever you have. Some are on the streets because life has given them no other choices. Some are there because it is safer or more comfortable for them than the places they left behind."

"Was she very young?" Royce asked.

"Twenty-six when she died."

Royce couldn't bring himself to ask the obvious question.

"She confided in Jasmine one night. She wanted so badly to have the child, but knew her health wasn't all it should be. It took her a lot of courage to go to the doctor. By then, the cancer was too far advanced for treatment, even if they could have done anything while she was pregnant. When Jasmine offered to take her in, she agreed with great reluctance. She'd been on the streets so long, but she knew she had to overcome her fears for her baby to live."

"So she lived with Jasmine's family before the birth?"

"And after," Francis confirmed. "Her health declined rapidly. But she was smart enough to make sure Rosie wouldn't end up on the streets. They'd barely finished the adoption process before she died."

Jasmine glanced their way. Her smile here had a different, softer quality. Instead of the take-charge woman he'd butted heads with, in this environment, her leadership abilities seemed to be subdued under a layer of compassion.

Francis cleared his throat, reengaging Royce's

attention. "All that to say, Jasmine has volunteered here for years, but she's also changed
her entire life to take care of someone in need.
There's no doubt she loves Rosie. Her entire
family loves her. But it was, and is, a huge sac-
rifice in one so young."

"Why are you telling me this?" Royce asked.
After all, this was technically a business meeting.

Francis studied him for a long moment, a
slight smile on his face. "Call it intuition or the
prompting of the Spirit, but something tells me
you need to know. Even if Jasmine is just your
event planner."

Why did that last statement sound more like
a question to Royce? And why was he trying to
fool himself into thinking he wasn't interested?

"What about the children here?" Royce asked,
eager to change the subject. He thought back to
the boys in the gym. He hadn't failed to notice
the worn lettering on their clothes and thinness
of the soles on their shoes—and remembered the
years that his own clothes had looked the same.
"Is there anything special they need?"

"Right now, just the usual things that they always need. We have families who fund scholarships for some of our regulars in the after-school programs for disadvantaged families. Those scholarships and donors are coordinated by the Jefferson family from Savannah."

The Jeffersons. Instead of filing that detail away to use to his own advantage, Royce felt gratitude wash over him. They were doing so much for these kids. How much of a difference would it have made to him, to his mother, if he'd had the opportunity to participate in an after-school program like they offered here?

"We do have some other special programs we would love funding for, but I don't want to appear greedy."

Royce waved away his words. "It's not greedy when I asked. I'll have my assistant contact you for more information, okay?"

Francis nodded. "Thank you again."

"It's my pleasure." And Royce had a feeling he was going to have to admit to Jasmine that he'd changed his point of view. He wanted to be more involved in this charity event now. That had probably been her whole point in bringing him here: educating him for far more than just being able to talk knowledgably about his event's charity.

She'd done a thorough job of it, too.

Sure enough, they'd barely made it to the sidewalk in front of the cars when she paused and said, "Not as bad as you thought, was it?"

He turned to face her where she leaned against the moss-covered retaining wall. "You enjoy being right, don't you."

"Only with you." She grinned, her sassy joy drawing him out of his shell and into the sheer life she exuded. He found he was beginning to like her energy and enthusiasm—very much.

He shook his head, knowing he was going crazy. But for once, he didn't care about losing control. "You're incredible, you know?"

"Not really."

Royce leaned in close, propping one hand against the wall next to her glossy black hair. He swallowed hard against the emotions welling up despite himself. "To prove to my father that my life was worth something, I pursued wealth that would far surpass his."

For the first time, he let himself reach over and touch her thick hair. "To prove that life was still worth living after your parents died, you dedicated yourself to your family and taking care of others."

He stepped closer, bringing their bodies together even though he knew he shouldn't. "In the eyes of most people, that's incredible. Especially me."

Then Royce let his logical brain take a hike and brought his lips down on hers. Her taste was just as exotic as her name. Royce's craving shifted into overdrive.

If he'd thought it would just be a quick peck, he was mistaken. Instead, his body pressed closer. His mouth opened over hers. Her lips left a slightly sweet taste on his tongue, but it was the heat inside that he sought.

The catch of her breath sent a streak of sensation through him. He wanted to explore all the ways he could make her react. All the hidden places on her body that would make her gasp and moan. But for now, he focused on the heat of her mouth and the sexiness of her response.

After long, exquisite moments, Royce forced himself to pull back. To regain control. To think about Jasmine instead of his own sorry self.

Which meant he couldn't bring himself to look into those gorgeous blue eyes to see exactly how he'd ruined everything.

Ten

How in the world was she supposed to act after that kiss?

As Jasmine waited for Royce outside the non-descript building that housed one of the hottest restaurants in Savannah, she tried to shut her brain down. But the question wouldn't go away.

Not even in the face of her curiosity about the restaurant. She'd never been to After Hours before today. Word in elite circles was that it was incredible, but Jasmine had never been able to afford to eat here. And, to her knowledge, they didn't cater events, so she'd let it slide off her radar.

But Royce had insisted he knew exactly what he wanted done with the food for the charity event, and After Hours was it. Since she didn't have to pry or coax the opinion from him, she'd let him lead.

"Are you ready?"

Jasmine jumped. Tightening her control, she forced herself to take a deep breath before turning toward Royce. "I'm not sure," she admitted.

Instead of leering, Royce faced her with a benign grin. He could have approached the situation any number of ways, considering how she'd sprinted for her car after he'd kissed her on Saturday, but he didn't appear to be messing with her.

Though there was something suspicious...

"What's so funny?" she demanded, hiding her embarrassment behind a sassy attitude.

"You," he admitted. "Seeing you off kilter is honestly a little fun."

She studied him a little closer, but still didn't see any signs of sexual innuendo. That was a relief, but she still had the urge to call him a brat. Even if Auntie would say it was unladylike.

Instead she let him lead her inside with a light

grip on her elbow. Being on his territory was fun, but not nearly as comfortable as being the one in control. His confident stride and barely there grin said he definitely knew it.

The closed restaurant was dark, though sunshine tried to peek in around the drawn blinds. The hushed emptiness was disconcerting, though as much as she hated to admit it, the darkness evoked a sense of intimacy.

This meeting didn't have the same strictly business feel that their previous ones had started out with, even if they had all ended up being out of the ordinary. Especially the last one—that kiss had changed everything for her.

Though she'd never admit it, even under threat of torture.

One of the tall silver doors at the back of the room swung open, revealing a tall, lanky guy in a white chef's coat. "Royce!"

"Marco." Royce stepped forward to shake the other man's hand with more enthusiasm than Jasmine had seen from him before. "Good to see you, buddy."

"I wouldn't miss this for the world."

"Marco, this is my event planner, Jasmine Harden."

The chef turned his smile in her direction. "Welcome to After Hours."

"Thank you for having us," she murmured, leaving out how she'd always wanted to see the inside of this place. Now didn't seem the time to fawn over something that was so far outside her middle-class budget. Instead, she tried to keep her demeanor as professional as possible.

"Why don't y'all come back into the kitchen first?" Marco asked.

Jasmine followed him, her heeled boots clicking against the Italian tile floor.

"Royce mentioned that you were unfamiliar with our restaurant," Marco said over his shoulder. "We serve fresh, local, organic food whenever possible. The focus here is a modern Mediterranean cuisine, though we can add some Latin influence, since I know Royce likes things spicy."

"Royce Brazier?" Jasmine asked, thinking of the by-the-book businessman she constantly butted heads with. "Are you sure?"

Marco simply laughed, even though Jasmine

was only half teasing. And she was pretty sure she could make out the hint of a blush stealing over Royce's fair cheeks, despite the darkness.

Not wanting to embarrass him further, or draw out any discussion over how "spicy" he might like things, Jasmine said, "I wasn't aware After Hours catered." They'd never been on her list before today.

Marco grinned. "That's because we don't."

Jasmine looked between the two men. "I'm not sure I understand."

"We don't actually cater here, but I told Royce I would help him out for this event."

Jasmine was already shaking her head. "That's not a good idea." The last thing she wanted was an inexperienced staff working her star event.

"Don't worry," Royce said. "Marco did plenty of catering during school and early in his career."

"And I'm strictly a food man these days. So I've already partnered with Geraldine's to handle the catering service and staffing. You've heard of her?" Marco asked.

"Yes. I've worked with her on several occasions." Knowing that the logistics were taken care of helped calm Jasmine's panic.

Royce nodded as if that settled everything. "Well," he said, "let's show Jasmine what we had in mind."

Jasmine glanced over at him in surprise. That conspiratorial look was back again. For good reason.

When it came to food, Royce showed that he had a few surprises up his sleeve over the next half an hour. Instead of sitting back and only asking a few questions, as he had throughout most of their other meetings, the catering discussion brought out a passion in Royce she'd never seen before...or rather, only seen once before.

She'd more than seen it when he'd pressed his lips against hers.

She watched in unabashed awe as they tossed around menu ideas involving lobster, truffles and exotic spices. Royce certainly knew gourmet food. Jasmine had very little to add except for a few tips and tricks she'd learned throughout all the events she'd executed over the last five years.

Before long, Marco was shooing them to a table in the main room so he could assemble some sample plates for them. Jasmine grinned at Royce as they were seated. "He doesn't have to do this. I have a feeling anything that comes out of that kitchen is gonna be incredible."

Royce shook his head. "I never turn down the chance to taste anything Marco wants to make for me."

"You seem to know each other well."

"Since we were kids. We grew up not far from each other."

Jasmine wasn't sure if she wanted to broach the subject of his childhood. To change the conversation from business to personal. Instead, she glanced around the elegantly stark room now that the lights had been turned up some.

"Is he the one who taught you so much about food?"

Royce only hesitated a moment before he said, "I learned to cook really young, because my mom was gone at all hours."

So much for avoiding the personal.

"She would also bring home leftovers from different events where she served. That's how I developed a taste for food that was far out of our budget."

"I can sympathize." Jasmine rarely sampled anything that could be labeled *cuisine*, except at her events. They were more of a down home food family.

Royce grinned. "I'll have to cook for you sometime."

Seriously? The guy could cook?

He must have read the thoughts on her face. "Let me guess. You thought I was only the order-in type."

"Instead of?"

"The mess-up-the-dishes-and-have-to-run-the-dishwasher type." He relaxed back into his chair. "I spend all day out. Believe it or not, cooking is very relaxing."

"Well...I wouldn't know," she admitted.

This time he was the one to look shocked. "You don't cook? I thought every good Southern girl cooked."

"I prefer to eat the fruits of someone else's labors, in this instance."

"Then this is perfect for you," Marco said as he approached across the room.

He deftly placed a couple of long, hand-glazed platters on the table, each filled with gorgeous little colorful morsels that smelled as good as they looked.

"Oh, my."

Royce glanced up at his friend. "I think she's sold without a single bite."

"Just wait until she tastes it," Marco said with a grin, then strode back toward the kitchen.

Jasmine surveyed the bounty. "I don't know what to try first."

"There's an art to it."

She raised a brow at him. This was the first time the tables had been turned—a nonbusiness situation where Royce gave *her* advice.

"Trust me?"

He waited for her nod before lifting a tiny lettuce leaf cradling what appeared to be a meat and vegetable mixture off one of the trays. "Start here."

Before she could lift a hand to take it from him, he'd brought the bite to her lips. Jasmine felt her smile disappear as she blinked. She could do this. She would remain professional.

Even though this felt far from professional.

She let her lips open. Just as she took the food into her mouth she glanced up and met the delicious heat of his stare. Their proximity reminded her of his kiss, his lips over hers. Talk about delicious.

Sudden flavor burst over her tongue. Cool, crisp lettuce. Spicy meat with an undertone of shrimp. A sweet drizzle that she couldn't quite identify. As she moaned, she could see a reflection of her own experience in his eyes. His grin said he knew exactly what she was tasting. He picked up a matching hors d'oeuvre and slid it between his lips.

"Just the right amount of sweet to balance the spice," he said after he swallowed. Lifting a wineglass from the tray, he washed the morsel down.

Jasmine did the same. Her inspection of the trays revealed several options for her next bite, but Royce knew exactly what he wanted her to have. Taste after taste, he walked her through the platters. Spicy butter glazed lobster skewers, meatballs spiced up with chorizo, jerk chicken mini-pizzas…her taste buds were in heaven.

"You were right," she admitted about halfway through.

Royce gave her the most suggestive look she'd ever seen on his face. "About what?"

"The food."

He feigned shock. "I did something right?"

"This time you did, smart aleck. This food will be the talk of the town for months after the event."

"Marco will be thrilled to hear it."

"But you won't."

He shrugged, sobering a little. "I really couldn't care one way or another. But if I can help him even a little with this, then I'll count it as a plus."

"That's a great thing to do."

He shrugged again, then searched the platter with renewed enthusiasm and chose another morsel. Jasmine thought she heard the buzz of a phone but couldn't bring herself to care as she helped herself to a hyped-up version of teriyaki steak that ravished her taste buds.

A good fifteen minutes later, Jasmine heard the phone buzzing again. This time it was accompanied by Royce's grimace. He pulled his cell phone from his pocket and read the texts. "It's Matthew."

For the first time, Jasmine wished that he would ignore his phone. For the first time, her reasons were personal.

The telltale buzz filled the space between them. Matthew wasn't giving up. "I have to go," Royce said.

For the first time, the regret in Royce's voice matched Jasmine's feelings.

"Too bad," she said, not caring that her voice had gone husky. "I was having fun."

His gaze met hers, bringing a return of the electric atmosphere from earlier. "Me, too."

"Isn't your business ever fun?" Deep down, she knew she was past the point of being strictly professional.

"I'm good at it," he finally answered. "But no. Business has never been fun...until now."

"So the ring is working!"

"No," Jasmine insisted, frowning at her youngest sister. "That is not what I said at all."

"Close enough."

Why had she even broached this topic? Jasmine should have known better. Her sisters—both of them—had a tendency to take a notion and run with it. Auntie presided over the scene from her recliner in the corner of the breakfast nook. The mischievous look on her face meant there would be no help coming from that direction.

"I don't know why I tell y'all anything," Jasmine complained. "It's just—" But the word *business* wouldn't move past the constriction in her throat. She crossed the kitchen to stir the big pot of soup on the stove. Willow had chosen the perfect dinner for a rainy Saturday.

Though the chatter continued behind her, Willow appeared at her side. "Are you okay?"

While confident and decisive, Willow was also very sensitive to others. No one was more willing to lend a helping hand when she saw someone who needed it.

Jasmine lowered her voice. "I just can't forget how he talked about learning to cook because his mother was never home. And about being named after his father's car."

She absently stirred the soup, watching chunks of veggies appear and disappear beneath the liquid surface. The lack of sunlight in the room left the green jewel in her ring lackluster; Jasmine still had the feeling the jewelry was mocking her.

"I don't know what this is, but Ivy's right—it's not just business anymore."

Ring or no ring.

Willow gave a tiny squeal that she quickly silenced under Jasmine's glare.

"What about him? What does he think?" Willow asked, echoing Jasmine's own questions.

She didn't want to admit that Mr. Business was turning out to be someone completely unexpected. Jasmine could never have guessed that the stern CEO she'd met in his office that first day would be able to melt her with such a hot kiss. But hadn't that tattoo on his neck hinted at hidden depths? A tattoo she had yet to see in its entirety, now that she thought about it.

"From your silence, I gather Royce is showing signs of moving in a different direction, too," Willow filled in for her.

"Surprisingly," Jasmine mused. "I think so."

"So why not just go with it?"

Jasmine gave the soup a final stir, then peeked into the oven at the cornbread sizzling in a cast-

iron skillet. It was a simple delaying tactic, since
they all knew cooking wasn't in her skill set.

"It's not that easy." She glanced over her shoulder to check on Rosie, who was cooing at Auntie and Ivy from her bouncy seat. "Even leaving
aside the fact that he's my boss...of sorts. How
can I get involved? Royce definitely isn't the
family type. I have Rosie..."

"She's six months old," Ivy said from right
behind them.

Jasmine jumped. "How'd you move that
quick?"

Ivy had a baby face, but her grin made her
look even younger. "I have my ways." She shook
her head, making her blond curls dance. "And
I wasn't about to miss what all the whispering
was about, now, was I?"

She linked her arm with Jasmine's and adopted
the expression of a captive audience. "Now's the
perfect time for you to live a little. Rosie isn't old
enough to notice at this age. Later, you'll need
to be more careful because she'll realize when
Mommy is gone or bringing someone to visit."

"I don't know." Everything about this change
in their attitudes toward each other had Jasmine

off kilter. She and Royce had sparred from the moment they met. But now, something different was emerging. Something she wasn't sure she was ready to face.

Willow nodded in agreement with Ivy, but Jasmine didn't want to concede that her baby sister was right. She searched for a reply that didn't make her look like a scaredy-cat. From across the room, Jasmine's ringtone filled the air.

"Sweetheart," Auntie called. "It's that nice young man from the hospital."

Jasmine shared a look with Willow. The temptation to ignore the call was strong. Jasmine wasn't ready for the test she could sense was coming around the corner.

"Why don't you answer it?" Ivy teased. "After all, it's just business."

"Brat."

Willow was less about talk than action. She simply herded Jasmine in the direction of her phone. Jasmine removed her apron as she went. She caught the call right before it switched to voice mail. As she answered, she was acutely aware of her audience.

"Hello?"

"Jasmine?"

Even his voice sounded different. The cadence a little slower. The tone a touch deeper. How was that possible? "Yes?"

"Since our tasting session was cut short, I thought I'd make it up to you by cooking dinner for you."

That was more like Royce—straight to the point. It was the nature of his point she couldn't quite grasp.

She could feel the eyes of everyone in the room staring at her. Even Rosie seemed to be watching, still and waiting for her answer to an unknown question. Jasmine hesitated. Going to Royce's penthouse was definitely not business. She glanced back and forth between Willow's encouraging expression and Ivy's excited one. Jasmine forced herself to turn away, to lay the burden of other people's expectations aside for once.

Even as she paced a few steps and opened her mouth to answer, she wasn't sure what to say. Was she ready for this? Probably not.

But then she thought over everything she'd been through in the last year. Learning Rosie's mother was pregnant, that she would probably die. Bringing her to live here. Taking care of her family while learning to be a mother for the first time. All while holding down a crazy job.

What the hell—it was time to live for once.

Eleven

Royce knew he was in trouble the minute Jasmine walked out of the elevator into the foyer in one of those feminine, flowy dresses she wore. Only this one seemed to have a little more oomph—a little extra cleavage, a slit up one side. Or was his overheated brain imagining that?

He felt like someone had flipped a switch inside him, jumpstarted an electrical pulse that shot through him whenever Jasmine was near. It was like the exhilaration of implementing a successful business plan—only a hundred times harder and sharper.

He didn't want to fight it anymore. Didn't want to fight her.

Make love, not war. Wasn't that a phrase from days past? His mother used to say it. Not that it had gotten her far. Her inability to go to war against his father had turned her life into endless days of drudgery—until Royce had stepped in to change that.

Royce opened the door to his penthouse to allow Jasmine inside. Her heels clicked on the glossy black tile. She breathed deep. "Something smells incredible," she said. Her slight smile intrigued him.

Was she nervous?

When she swallowed, it confirmed his suspicions, though he had to look hard to notice. "You weren't kidding that you could cook," she said.

"I just need to finish a few last-minute things. You aren't averse to any particular seafood, are you?"

She shook her head, bringing his attention to the thick dark hair swinging around her shoulders.

"That's good, or else this would be a complete disaster," he said with a laugh that seemed to break the unexpected tension between them. "I'm finishing up some shrimp scampi. The sides and salad are ready. But I wimped out on the dessert."

"Not you," Jasmine mocked in her sassy way.

"I'm not a pastry chef. I figured since we didn't make it to dessert the other day, I'd go by Marco's and pick up a praline cheesecake."

The O of her mouth was encouraging—and sexy as hell. "Sounds awesome," she said. "But I'm surprised you would admit you can't cook everything."

"I realized a long time ago that there was no point in pretending to be something I'm not."

Her delectable body went still for mere seconds, but Royce caught it. He should have expected a question to follow.

"Was it a problem? Early on?"

He waved her farther into the living area as thoughts swirled through his mind. He watched her take in the comfortably luxurious space. Royce had never wanted to live in a showplace. A few designers had tried to convince him otherwise, but eventually he'd found someone who understood his preferences. The magnificent space was in one of Savannah's formerly dilapidated shipping warehouses, now refurbished for people who could afford the best—although his "best" meant an awesome sound system, over-stuffed leather furniture and a magnificent view. Not high-priced works of art and anemic, un-comfortable chairs.

Jasmine seemed to agree. "Wow," she breathed as she approached the wall of windows looking out toward downtown and the river.

The architect had pushed out the walls so the floor extended all the way to the stone arches that used to frame an old balcony for ship watch-ing. The arches were now fitted with glass panes for an extended view from inside the unusual room.

"This is an incredible blend of old and new," she said. "I'm very impressed."

"It's relaxing when I finally make it home at night."

The black mirrored tile from the foyer gave way to glossy wood floors in the living areas. Royce walked over to the bar in the far corner. "Having you here gives me a chance to use the bar. I hardly ever have company."

He fixed the martini she requested while she strolled along the long wall of windows, skirted the corner bar and continued along the shorter wall. "Incredible."

"Thank you."

"And thank you for inviting me here." This time her look was more straightforward, promising.

Royce felt his insides heat up. "Well, thanks to you, I'm learning to mix business with pleasure."

She lifted the martini glass in salute. "Me, too."

If he let this go much farther, dinner would be burned beyond recognition. "I'd better finish up the food."

As he turned away, he heard her footsteps behind him. "Mind if I join you?"

He paused, giving her a chance to catch up. "Please feel free."

As they walked down a short corridor and into his designer kitchen, he had to chuckle.

"What's so funny?" she asked.

"I just realized." He paused, then let a long, slow breath ease out, surprised he was admitting this. "I just realized that, besides my mother and the cleaning lady, you are the first person to ever join me in my kitchen."

"Wow. Really?"

He watched as her blue gaze roamed over the mahogany cabinets with their black hardware, the cream ceramic appliances and the black tile on the walls. She made a beeline for the stools on the other side of the kitchen island. The large room was designed for social gatherings, but Royce had never used it as such.

"Yes," he murmured. "Really."

But what was even odder was how comfortable he felt with her in his space, if comfortable was even the word to describe the electrical connection that continued to surprise him.

But it wasn't the only thing that surprised him. He was also bemused by how completely at ease they were with each other. They ended up eating at the island in the kitchen, seated across from each other on stools. Her eyes sparkled just as much as her wineglass under the lights. Their conversation flowed naturally from the upcoming masquerade to other events they'd attended.

After exclaiming over the food with genuine enthusiasm, Jasmine took her wineglass and wandered back down the hallway to the living room. Night had taken full hold. The mature trees below and the climbing ivy overflowing the outer walls onto the windowsills gave the impression of being protected by nature as they looked onto the lights spread out before them. Savannah was a city of hard brick and lush greenery. "It really is beautiful, Royce." She half turned toward him. "I can't believe your mother loved the manor house more."

"She did enjoy the view here, but I think Keller House made her think of a time when she was happier, when life had possibilities."

Jasmine was nice enough to add, "But in the end, she was left with the knowledge that she had raised a fully capable young man who would take care of himself and her."

He glanced down into his glass, feeling a familiar mixture of sadness and pride. "She didn't have to worry anymore."

Suddenly he felt a brush of warmth on his arm. Through his dress shirt, he could feel the outline of Jasmine's hand. He couldn't count the number of times recently he had dreamed of how soft her skin would be against his. How those perfectly manicured nails would feel against his back. Or how the curves of her body would feel pressed against his.

She was offering comfort. He needed to remind himself of that.

Then she stepped closer. Any effort at restraint became exponentially harder. He allowed himself a glance, only to find her gaze locked on him. And it wasn't overflowing with sympathy. With just one look they both knew exactly where this was headed. "Will you stay the night?" he finally asked.

"Do you really need to ask?"

That amused him. "Sweetheart, with you I never assume anything."

Her smile was a concession to everything they'd been through so far. "Then let me make myself plain. Assume all you want."

Royce may have been cautious about getting to a more intimate stage, but when the time came, Jasmine found he was as focused in the bedroom as he was in the boardroom.

One minute they were facing each other, then he took a few purposeful steps to bring her within reach. She barely had time to blink before Royce's hand was in her hair and his mouth once more covered hers. The heat that she remembered from their first kiss was there, this time underpinned by a purpose that made her insides melt.

He tasted spicy, which ramped up the temperature inside her. There was nothing tentative about his kiss. Instead, he conquered her with smooth glides and strong pulls. There was nothing more for her to do than enjoy.

When he pulled back, she was tempted to beg him not to stop, but she clamped her teeth over her lower lip to keep the words inside. Her body was anxious, aching for the race to be finished. But Jasmine wanted to savor the ride. She glanced up to find his gaze glued to the deep V of her neckline—a design she'd deliberately chosen with him in mind.

Then her own gaze dropped and she glimpsed the edges of his neck tattoo above the open collar of his button-down shirt. Curious, she let her fingers trail over the skin of his neck to push the material aside.

To her surprise, the elegant tendrils she'd often glimpsed above his collar gave way to a solid shield, an old-world symbol emblazoned with a brilliantly colored dragon. It stood for strength. Protection. Not what she'd expected, but somehow very fitting for the man she was coming to know.

Her smile gave him all the permission he needed. His palms slid from the back of her neck down over her collarbones, leaving warm trails that quickly faded. When he finally reached her breasts, she gasped. Her nipples tightened in a quick rush, eager for attention.

He simply held them, each mound a handful. The heat from his hands soaked into her skin through the layers of her clothing. She couldn't stop her back from arching just a little. Then his thumbs began a dedicated exploration that made her wish her clothes would just disappear.

She had no recollection of ever needing someone to see her, touch her, this badly. It was scary—just as much as it was exhilarating.

After long, long moments of exquisite torture, his devilish hands moved down—tracing her generous curves. His touch wasn't simple. No. It was magic. The pressure and heat imprinted the feel of him on her skin.

How could a seemingly innocent touch make her knees go weak? Cause her bones to melt until she leaned forward, her hands braced on his shoulders as he knelt before her?

He eased off one of her high-heeled pumps. His thumbs traced the line of her foot before he squeezed hard into the arch, surprising a gasp from her. Maintaining the pressure, he slid his fingers along the silky surface of her thigh-highs. Too soon, he reached underneath her skirt to find the tops of her stockings and roll them down her legs.

Who knew being undressed could be such a sensual dance?

By the time both legs were bare, Jasmine's entire body throbbed. Royce looked up at her from his crouching position. "Take your dress off for me."

She knew where every tie was, every clasp. But she kept her movements slow, taking her time, building anticipation. It was worth ignoring her own need to see his eyes widen as she revealed a pale pink, lace-edged slip over matching bra and panties. When the dress finally puddled at her feet, he gripped her silk-covered hips and buried his face against her.

She thought she heard him suck in a deep breath. His hands tightened for a moment. Her tummy quivered beneath his cheek. Her throat went dry while she grew slick between her thighs.

Royce stood, only pulling his hands away at the very last minute. That small concession told her more than anything that he wanted her as much as she wanted him. Then he circled around her to take in the view from every angle. To her surprise, he turned her to face the window. That's when she realized their reflections stared back as if from an antique mirror. Hazy. Shimmery.

"This," he said, running a finger along one bra strap, then the lace that edged the top curve of one breast, "is very sexy." He pulled the straps down off her shoulders. Then he hooked his fingers in the material of her slip and slowly eased it down over her curves. "But it isn't what I'm most interested in seeing."

She had only a moment to catch the reflection of herself in the bra and panties before he picked her up and carried her down a longer hallway to the back of the penthouse.

With a quick sweep of her gaze, she took in the dim bedroom with dark furniture and smoky walls before Royce arranged her on the comforter on her knees, facing him as he stood beside the bed. The soft moonlight from the bedroom windows revealed his outline, but the details of his expression were now lost to her. Once more he traced the edges of the clothes she had left before slipping his hands beneath the silk of her panties to cup her rear.

His touch was firm, with just enough concession to her softness. Pulling her close, he rubbed his fully clothed body against her. The fact that he was covered while she was practically naked left her feeling decadent. The pressure of his erection excited her. Her body went wet in anticipation.

Again, that firm grip guided her down until she lay on the bed. His mouth devoured hers, teeth nipping her lips, tongue delving inside to stroke against hers.

She lost herself in the sensations.

Then, somehow, his mouth was sucking at

her naked breast, pulling cries from her straining lungs. He worked one nipple, then the other until they were tight and hard. Electrical pulses streaked through her. She lifted her pelvis against him, more than ready for some relief from the driving urges inside her body.

Deftly, Royce rose to his knees. His dress shirt was gone in seconds. He opened his pants to reveal the very thing she needed in this moment. He put on protection quickly, efficiently. Then, with a snap of his wrist, he broke through her panties. All barriers were gone. Finally his body covered hers.

She could feel the rub of his suit pants against the insides of her thighs as his body searched for her opening. His fingers spread her wide, coating her with her own moisture to ease the way. Then they teased her, drawing out her cries of desperation.

Not soon enough, he entered her. She struggled for a moment to accommodate him. The pressure was exquisite. One lift of her hips and he slid inside.

There was no more waiting, no more savoring. They were both too desperate.

She clutched at his ribs as he pistoned into her, demanding her response. Indulging his own. Her cries mingled with his groans in the darkness.

All too soon, she needed more. Needed his utmost. She dug her nails into his buttocks, urging him to give her everything.

Then the exquisite pressure burst. The world turned white in a shower of stars. But the best part of it all was knowing that he followed her.

Twelve

Royce woke to movement on the other side of the bed. He opened his eyes. Though there weren't any lights on, he could see Jasmine walk around the end of the bed and out the door to the hallway. It was 1:30 a.m.

The normal debate he'd expect to have with himself never occurred. He simply acknowledged that he had no desire for Jasmine to leave. Getting up, he took a few seconds to pull on a pair of boxers—more for her comfort than his. Then he followed her to the living room.

He located her in one corner near the window by the light of her phone. She seemed to be reading from the screen. As he got closer, he could see that she'd pulled on her slip. Just the thought of that silky material over her naked skin sent him spinning.

Now he knew how someone could become addicted after just one hit.

"Everything okay?" he asked softly, hoping not to scare her.

She only jumped a little. Then she shook her head. "Yeah. I was just checking in."

The silence hung between them for a minute, but for Royce it wasn't the usual awkwardness that came with this situation. Though he could honestly say he'd never been in this situation before. He'd never fallen asleep next to any of the few women he'd bothered to let distract him enough from work to get to sex. Now he couldn't think of anything he wanted more than for Jasmine to spend the rest of the night.

That should have had him freaking out, but he wasn't going to analyze why it didn't.

"Need to go?" he finally asked.

Jasmine hesitated. If he'd been in her situation, he would have, too. Honestly, there was no way she could possibly imagine him wanting her to stay. After all, look at his past behavior.

Covering the few steps left between them, Royce let his body act on instinct. He reached out and cupped the cool skin of her upper arms. Then he rubbed up and down, aiming to warm her. But also to fulfill his own craving to simply touch her.

She stared up at him in the dark. Beneath his touch she shivered, then she shook her head.

For him, the answer was simple. "Then come back to bed."

When they got back to the bed, that first touch of skin on skin exhilarated him. He rolled over her, covering her cool body with his warmth. Savoring the gasp of air that signaled her surrender.

Royce moaned against her neck, opening his mouth to feel her pulse against his tongue. Her taste was unique, almost floral, but sweet, too. His body responded by hardening, and he reached for her. *Holy smokes.*

"You are like a gourmet meal for me alone."

Jasmine arched against him. He breathed her in, nipping her ear and burying his hands in her hair. This time he savored her touch, too. The feel of her palms grazing down his sides. The light scrape of her nails across his ass. The softness of her lips beneath his.

Her legs slid apart, making a home for him between them. He rubbed himself against her most sensitive spot, wanting to shout because she was so wet for him.

Lifting himself a little, he regretted the space he had to create, if only for a moment. Quickly he covered himself with a condom, then worked his way inside of her. So tight. Incredibly hot. There was no way he could wait.

He was overcome with an instinct to imprint her with his scent, his touch, in case she ever thought she could walk away. Where the possessive urges came from, he had no idea. They were unique to Jasmine. He couldn't resist.

As he gave his first long, slow thrust, he rubbed his body up hers. Never had full body contact felt so good. He felt her slick skin, alert nipples, harsh breath. Most of all, the clasp of her around him.

He anchored his hands in her hair. Then he started to thrust in earnest. The strain in his thighs, the twist of his hips, didn't seem to be enough. Her nimble legs encircled his hips, urging him to thrust harder. Faster.

He attuned his senses to her body's responses. Not just her breath and the lift of her hips, but the subtle clutch of her muscles around his hardness. He nurtured every hint of ecstasy until she called his name in the darkness. They worked together until Royce thought his heart would explode. But he couldn't let go until she did.

Shifting his angle, he ground against the soft cushion of her mound with his pelvis. Her breath caught. Her neck arched. Her hold on him tightened. Then there was the extra force that threw her over the edge.

Her incredible cries filled his ears as her body clamped down hard and milked him dry. There was no denying the demand for him to join her.

Now or ever again.

"I haven't seen you in three days," Royce pointed out. With some men, the reminder would have been a whine. With him, it was a simple logical statement. Until he got to the question. "Are you trying to tell me something?"

In this instance, the complications were all on

Jasmine's side. Not Royce's. Most men would have been trying to find ways to keep a woman at arm's length. Not this time.

Much to her surprise.

She wanted to sigh as she glanced over the planner on the desk before her. She wished it wasn't overflowing with Willow's classes, Ivy's job and blocks of time that she really needed a sitter for Rosie. Facts were facts. She should have known life would interfere with the blissful two weeks she'd spent exploring the incredibly sensual side of Royce Brazier—but she couldn't keep business and her personal life separate forever.

She'd never been good at juggling.

But *business* wasn't even the right word. What she and Royce were doing in the luxurious bedroom of his penthouse had nothing to do with business. Still, she was doing her best to keep him and her family far away from each other. Royce had made it clear he wasn't in the market for a family. She was a single woman with a small child. The last thing she wanted was for him to think she was daddy hunting.

For a man like him, the title of *daddy* would never be an option.

"I just can't get away tonight." The planner clearly showed that Willow had a night class to teach. And Ivy had called to say she would probably be working late that night. Auntie was recovering nicely, but her abilities and stamina with a small child were limited. This left Jasmine between a rock and...well, a very lonely, needy place.

Royce hesitated for only a moment. "Would your family object to me dropping by?"

"Why would you?"

Silence greeted her unexpected question, but only for a moment. Just long enough for her to feel mortified.

"Believe it or not, Jasmine," Royce said, without any of the angry heat she would have expected, "I do enjoy more about you than just the sex."

Jasmine almost choked.

"And they have met me before," he reminded her.

Not as a potential suitor. At least, in her eyes. This visit just might confirm what her family was expecting…except Jasmine knew her liaison with Royce could never live up to the romantic fantasy they would build in their minds.

When she finally answered, her voice sounded small. "It just didn't occur to me you would want to come by."

"Jasmine." His voice deepened, almost a reflection of the turmoil rumbling around inside of her. "I'm finding, to my surprise, that I'll take you any way I can get you."

Royce always was one to tell the truth, whether the other person wanted to hear it or not. The sheer enormity of his confession shut her up quick. They agreed on a time for him to drop by.

The bewilderment and need in his voice were still eliciting tremors later that evening as she waited for him to arrive. Mostly because they echoed her own feelings.

She found her attachment to Royce too close for comfort. Her craving for him only grew each time they were together. She wanted to bounce ideas off him at odd times. She even wished she could spar with him on occasion. Talking to him. Cooking with him. Making love with him. He never failed to stimulate her in some way—in all the ways that mattered.

But he wasn't a family man—had no desire to ever be one. So her need for him to be more than he could offer scared her more than anything.

Her hands still shook as she opened the door that evening. It should have been a scene from a romantic movie—a handsome man on her doorstep with blooming trees filling the background behind him as the sun set. Instead, it could have been the boogeyman at her door, if her feelings of trepidation were to be believed.

"Hey," she greeted him, her voice hushed.

"Hey, yourself." He matched his tone to hers as he glanced behind her. "Are we having a secret liaison on your doorstep or is there something I need to know?"

That would have been funny if she hadn't actually been keeping her family in the dark as much as possible since that night two weeks ago. Still, she tried for an amused grin, ignoring her nerves.

"No. Auntie and Rosie fell asleep."

Letting him in, she gestured toward the entrance to the family room, where Auntie could be seen lying propped up with lots of pillows on the couch. Rosie reclined against her, pacifier in place, blanket snuggled close. There was a cartoon on the TV turned to a low volume.

"They were watching television together. But Rosie seems to have caught Auntie's tendency to take cat naps now that she's having to rest her leg so much."

Royce studied the sleeping pair, though Jasmine couldn't read his expression. "She looks peaceful."

She assumed he meant Rosie. "She's a good baby. I'm very, very lucky."

He turned back. "So am I, hopefully."

Jasmine raised an eyebrow. "Trust me. There's not enough time for sex."

Royce quickly smothered a laugh. "I guessed that much. But is a proper hello too much to ask for?"

Jasmine's cheeks burned. Shame on her for accusing him of only having sex on the brain.

Leading the way to the kitchen at the back of the house, she busied herself putting coffee on to perk. Anything to give her blush a chance to subside. She'd learned that Royce was an avid coffee drinker. Caffeine didn't seem to faze him. He drank it at all hours of the day—not that he slept much, anyway.

Only after the task had distracted her from her embarrassment did she cross the room and kiss him. It was a little more than a peck, but not much more before she pulled back. "How was your day?"

Dang it. Though she'd asked him that before, in this setting it took on a different connotation. More of a "How was your day, dear?" connotation.

"The Jeffersons have received my proposal." He grimaced, staring off into space for a moment. That tiny frown between his brows when he focused on something was unexpectedly sexy. "I hope they find everything in order."

"How can they not, with all the hard work you and your assistant put into this? And the masquerade will be fabulous. You're definitely gonna be noticed."

Even though she doubted he needed one, she gave him a hug. Her entire family were huggers. It served as greeting, comfort, reassurance, encouragement, celebration—like a language all its own. She and Ivy had talked at length about the difficulties of being a hugger in a business setting. It was a hard habit to shut off.

Finally, she leaned back to look at him. "Besides, I got good news today."

"What's that?" His voice had gone husky, warning her he was losing interest in business and moving on to far more interesting topics.

She couldn't help but smile. As much as she knew she shouldn't—she loved the effect she had on him. "I received an invite to the Sunday Salon yesterday. We attend on the fifteenth."

"Yes, ma'am. I'll be there with bells on, as my mama used to say." She couldn't help but notice that, even though the words were right, his eyes were trained on her lips.

"That would make a memorable fashion statement," she murmured, just before his lips found hers.

They'd just reached the gasping-and-fumbling-with-clothes stage when Jasmine heard a whimper from the other room. She stiffened.

Pulling back, Royce straightened his tie, then took a deep breath. "I'll just fix myself a cup of coffee," he said.

Leaving him to fend for himself, Jasmine rushed to the living room where Auntie was still snoring softly and Rosie was rubbing her eyes.

After picking the baby up and soothing her with a soft swaying motion for a moment, Jasmine headed back to the kitchen, not wanting to disturb the older woman's rest. Auntie hadn't slept well since her fall. Simply finding a comfortable way to sit or lie down could be a challenge on the bad days.

As soon as she stepped into the kitchen, Jasmine ran into another problem. Rosie stiffened a moment when she noticed the unidentified male in the room. But it didn't bother her for long.

Jasmine was in the process of saying, "You remember Mr. Royce, don't you?" when the little girl threw her whole body forward in a swan dive. Right in Royce's direction. The move was so unexpected that Jasmine wasn't able to get a good grasp. Rosie would have slipped from her arms if Royce hadn't stepped forward and caught Rosie.

Jasmine didn't know if it had been instinct for him, but it saved her daughter from what could have been a nasty tumble to the tile floor.

As soon as she'd caught her breath, Jasmine exclaimed, "Oh, goodness. I don't know how that happened." Her panicked mind replayed the child's jump for Royce over and over.

"No problem," he said, sounding far calmer than she felt. He immediately righted the baby and positioned her in his arms as if it were something he did on a daily basis.

All Jasmine could do was blink and breathe.

Rosie, the little stinker, ignored the drama she'd caused her mama and immediately began to babble at her captive audience. Royce's colorful tie seemed to fascinate her. And Jasmine could swear the baby was actually flirting as she glanced up at Royce's face and bestowed a big, gummy grin on him.

It might have been funny if it was anyone but Royce. The man who wanted nothing to do with family.

"Here. I'll take her," Jasmine offered with a step forward.

"It's fine," he assured her.

Unsure what else to do, she waved toward the table. "Have a seat."

As he settled them in at the dining room table,

Jasmine brought his forgotten coffee from the counter. She stood next to them for a moment, fascinated and embarrassed by her daughter's animated behavior—and Royce's ability to take it all in stride. When had this happened?

Before she could get a handle on the scene before her, Jasmine was mortified to hear her sister Ivy say from behind her, "Well, isn't this the perfect picture of domesticity?"

Thirteen

This was not how Royce had planned to spend his evening. Very few men would complain about being surrounded by a roomful of beautiful Southern women, being served delicious home cooking—and Royce wasn't going to be the one to start.

He'd simply planned to spend it with Jasmine. Alone. Preferably naked.

It took considerable self-control not to watch her every move with a hungry gaze, though baby Rosie's attachment to him had dampened his ardor significantly, as had the avid speculation on the other women's faces. He wasn't sure what was up with the little squirt, but she'd apparently decided Royce was her one and only adult tonight. She wasn't having it any other way. Any time Jasmine or her sisters tried to hold Rosie or move her away from him, big tears flooded her little eyes and rolled down her cheeks.

Much to his chagrin, Royce was a sucker for it.

Her high chair had been set beside him with Jasmine on the other side. The setup felt unreal to him, as if his brain couldn't comprehend what he'd gotten himself into. But he also had no desire to hightail it for the front door—an odd development, to say the least.

Normally, he would have been the first one to hit the road.

As they ate, Rosie alternated between her baby food and sippy cup, and playing with the emerald ring on Jasmine's right hand.

"You wear that ring a lot," he said. "Where's it from?"

The table went strangely silent, as if he'd asked something completely inappropriate—or something they didn't really want to answer.

"It's an heirloom piece we recently found in an old jewelry box," Auntie finally said.

Royce could swear the women around him slumped just a little.

"The girls' family line goes all the way back to the origins of Savannah. Their ancestor was a pirate who turned respectable and married the daughter of one of the founding families."

Royce grinned at Jasmine over Rosie's head. "Respectable, huh? So that's where you learned to fit in with the elite crowd so well."

"It's in the genes," she confirmed, putting on a fake bravado.

"It's actually quite fascinating," Willow said before launching into a monologue about Savannah's origins.

"History nerd," Jasmine mumbled out of the side of her mouth.

Royce quickly smothered his laugh when Willow glared. "I would hope so," she declared. "Otherwise I'd suck at teaching it."

"That makes perfect sense," Royce said. "I'm sure someone who loves history makes it much more interesting for her students."

That seemed to mollify Willow—that and sticking her tongue out at her sister.

Royce felt himself relaxing even more. Dinner

around the family table was an experience he'd never had. When he and his mother had eaten together, usually on Sundays, they'd sat next to each other in front of the television, eating off of TV trays. He hadn't expected to enjoy this when he'd sat down tonight.

Just then, a soft weight rested against his arm. He glanced down into the two soft brown eyes in Rosie's tiny round face. She blinked slowly, then rubbed her head against his arm.

"Um…" Royce glanced around the table, something akin to panic building in his core.

Willow giggled first, then Ivy. Auntie simply smiled.

Jasmine rolled her eyes, shaking her head at her daughter. "You big flirt."

"She is a woman, after all," Auntie said.

Royce glanced back down. The baby grinned, showing the first of her teeth in her otherwise empty gums. The panic disintegrated. A feeling he didn't recognize settled in its place. Something similar to how he felt when lying exhausted in Jasmine's arms. Almost like…peace.

"How about a change of subject?" Jasmine asked. "After all, I'm not sure how comfortable I am thinking about my six-month-old as a woman. Too early." She turned to Royce. "Shall we talk about the Jeffersons' soirée?"

"Oh, you get to go to that?" Ivy asked. "I loved the times I was allowed to go as Jasmine's guest."

Willow frowned. "Not me. Too many people and I had no idea what to talk about. I much prefer smaller groups."

"Which is why I'm going to the masquerade and you aren't," Ivy said.

"Have fun." Obviously Willow was not the social butterfly type.

Jasmine explained, "Willow is more of an introvert than the rest of us."

"My students are about as big of a group as I can handle," Willow said. "And even that exhausts me sometimes."

"I can sympathize, Willow," Royce said. "I'm a homebody myself. Comfortable only in my private spaces or the office. I don't often attend social events, but when I do, I try to think of these things as business meetings—just with more people present and a more fluid agenda."

"I hate to burst your bubble, but not this time," Jasmine said.

Royce glanced at her over the baby hugging his arm. "What do you mean?"

Her blue eyes were slightly somber. "The Jeffersons don't do business at these things. It's very socially oriented. That's why they are picky about the guest list."

"All of these social events are covers for getting business done. You may not see it, but it's there," Royce insisted. He'd been to enough of them to know, even if such parties weren't his preferred venue. "Otherwise, they'd be a big waste of time."

She was already shaking her head. "Not this time. While there are usually a lot of business people there, it isn't discussed directly. Remember my little talk about building connections, not just business deals? They're just as important. Trust me."

"Sure." *We'll see.* Jasmine was a smart woman. A whole lot more people smart than he was. But Royce knew business...and he was determined to advance his at every opportunity—no matter what she thought she knew.

Royce would trust his instincts. Every time.

Jasmine smoothed out the collar of her dress, then the skirt. It felt weird to be heading to a public event with Royce. They'd spent plenty of time together in private—delectable time. And, yes, they'd occasionally talked business or gone over progress for the masquerade, but this was different. Something they had never addressed.

Attending the Jeffersons' Sunday Salon with Royce put her on a path that left her with no distinct sense of how to act. Was this business? Was it a date? Would she look into his eyes and see the heat that often exploded between them without warning?

How should she react? Naturally? Or keep it under wraps? All the questions had her twisting her hands together in her lap.

Suddenly Royce pulled his car over and put it in park. Jasmine's stomach flip-flopped. But she swallowed against the tightening in her throat and asked, "Is something wrong?"

"You tell me. *Is* something wrong, Jasmine?"

"How did you know?" As if her stiffness this morning wasn't a clear sign. She'd been hoping he would ignore it.

"You're not at all your normal happy, mischievous self today."

She glanced over at him, realizing that was probably the first time she'd looked directly at him since they'd gotten into the car. No wonder he'd asked. Royce wasn't stupid.

"Sorry."

"Just tell me what it is and we'll figure it out."

He was right. Even though this was the last thing she wanted to talk about, what was the point of prolonging the torture that she'd been enduring for over a month? "I'm just not sure…" She swallowed, trying to loosen up her throat. This was something she'd never had to say to a client. "I'm not sure how you want me to act while we are here…out in public."

His grip tightened on the steering wheel as he nodded slowly. "I see what you mean."

"I know you hired me as your event planner. Attending this party was part of our business agreement. I'm just—"

Without warning, he leaned across the console to cup her face with his palms. The press of his lips to hers was so familiar now, almost as necessary as breathing. The fear, the uncertainty sparked by that revelation, was something she spent a lot of energy ignoring every day.

She opened her eyes to meet his, just inches away.

"I should have known this would be a problem," he murmured.

Her heart sank.

"I have no idea where this is going between us," Royce said.

This was it…he was going to dump her because she'd asked how he wanted her to behave in public.

He rubbed his thumb against her cheek. "But it's time we just accept that it's there and deal with it. Don't you agree?"

"Wait. What?"

"Surprised?" He granted her his rare grin. "Me, too."

As if he couldn't stop himself, he kissed her again. His touch was tinged with a gentleness that had tears burning behind her eyes.

"Listen," he said. "We don't have to be all over each other. We don't have to ignore what's happening between us, either."

Jasmine took a deep breath, searching his expression. "You don't care if people talk?"

"My mom and I learned a long time ago that talk can't hurt you if you don't let it. You and I started on this path with business as the sole purpose, but we left that behind a while back."

She sat stunned while he pulled back out onto the road. She'd been working hard to convince herself that her time with Royce was limited and would eventually end. That he could never accept Rosie or Jasmine's commitment to her family. All to keep herself from getting too involved.

He'd been so accepting of Rosie the other night. Jasmine hadn't tested it further, but seeing her daughter cuddle up to Royce's arm had done something to her. Made her wonder, for the brief moment she'd allowed herself to, whether this might actually be a possibility. Could this be another sign that what was happening between them might actually work? For real?

Silence reigned until they pulled into the long drive to the Jeffersons' palatial home. They lined up behind the considerable number of cars already parked out front.

It wasn't until Royce came around to help her out that he spoke. And he was so relaxed, it was as if there hadn't been a long silence between them. "So, you just be your beautiful, smart self, and I promise not to accost you when everyone is looking. Okay?"

"What about when they aren't?"

Again he reached out to her cheek, smoothing the pad of his thumb across it as if testing the texture of her skin. She heard the telltale note in his voice that always signaled his arousal as he said, "I'm sorry. I can't make any promises about that."

For the first time since she'd woken up that morning, Jasmine laid her worry aside and smiled. "I guess I'll have to live with that."

It was different, entering the stately house on Royce's arm. She'd been there over a dozen times before, and the Jeffersons had never made her feel anything but welcome. They did the same this time. Still, her smile was a little bigger, her confidence a little higher and her mood a whole lot brighter. Royce stiffened as they went in, but she chalked it up to adrenaline. She doubted Royce ever really felt nerves. But something had to power him through all those business negotiations and decisions.

"Royce Brazier, this is Don and Marilyn Jefferson, our hosts," she said, automatically attempting to put everyone at ease.

The man she'd respected for a long time shook Royce's hand without hesitation. "Welcome to our home. I believe we've met once or twice before, but always on more formal occasions," Don Jefferson said with his slow Southern drawl.

Jasmine was grateful to see Royce meet his gaze and shake his hand without any of the macho posturing she'd had to endure in some Savannah circles. "I believe so, sir. Thank you for having me."

"Always a pleasure. We're glad to see you, but would welcome anyone Miss Jasmine cared to bring with her."

"It was gracious of her to include me in her invite, sir," Royce said, with a smile in her direction that lingered just a little longer than normal.

Jasmine warmed from the inside out, despite the sleeveless summer dress she wore.

"This is my wife, Marilyn. Please, call me Don. Now Jasmine, why don't you show Royce where the food is? Make yourself at home. We can talk after a while," Mr. Jefferson said.

Fifteen minutes of mingling, with Royce's hand at the small of her back and a mimosa or two, helped Jasmine get a handle on how to behave. She let Royce lead, but introduced him to a few couples he hadn't met before. Most were familiar with his meteoric rise in Savannah's shipping industry but were gracious enough not to grill him on his presence at today's party.

"So, what are you working on now?" Evette Pierce asked Jasmine. She'd been to several of Jasmine's events, and they'd worked together on a charity event last spring.

"It's gonna be so much fun." Jasmine knew she was gushing, but she couldn't hold her excitement in. "We're working on a masquerade night in late May. You'll love it."

"Sounds fascinating."

"It will be. And the proceeds will go to build a dormitory for the mission."

Evette raised her wineglass. "A cause very

close to you, I know. You can count on me being there."

As they moved away, Royce leaned closer to whisper, "I thought this wasn't the place to discuss business?"

"She asked," Jasmine said with a shrug. "Besides, it wasn't really business. I was just passing her information about something fun I think she would enjoy."

"Po-*tay*-toes, pot-*ah*-toes."

She simply grinned. "Told you. Everything has a social spin."

"And you are the smarty-pants I should trust to know what she's doing?"

"Every time."

Royce grinned down at her. Movement in the doorway behind him caused her to glance over his shoulder. Don and Marilyn were greeting a man in the foyer. Suddenly Don looked toward her, a frown on his face as his gaze met hers. Only as the other man faced her did she realize who it was. And why Don looked so unhappy.

The man who had just arrived was Royce's father.

Fourteen

"I do want to apologize for the mix-up," Don said as he led Royce down an ornately paneled hallway into an office.

"What mix-up?" Royce asked.

Don let the heavily carved door close then studied Royce for a moment. He had a feeling this wasn't going to be a very comfortable conversation. And he could think of only one subject that would warrant this type of formality from his host.

"Of having your father here without any warning."

Bingo.

Don stepped into the room, gesturing Royce toward a chair while he took the one behind the large desk. "Not all of our guests are as courteous as Jasmine about letting us know who they are bringing with them."

Royce felt the unease that had been simmering since he'd first caught sight of his father rise a little higher. Not for himself, but— "I don't like the idea of him having access to Jasmine." Especially without him there to run interference.

Don offered an approving look. "We agree. Marilyn will be watching over her until you return. I assure you, she's quite capable of handling men of his ilk." He grinned. "Jasmine can, too, though she's often polite to a fault."

He studied Royce for a minute more before he asked, "Does he know about the two of you?"

"What?"

"That your relationship has become personal as well as professional?"

Royce wasn't sure he wanted to address that issue yet. Something had been bothering him since this conversation started.

"How did you know he was my father?" Royce asked. "That's not something I advertise."

"I don't blame you. He's not the kind of man I'd want to claim as a relation, either."

Royce met the other man's gaze in surprise. It wasn't often he had conversations with people who would admit to disliking his father as much as he did.

Don explained. "I'm a very thorough man. I know a lot about you, Royce. I've kept you on my radar for a while. With your meteoric rise on Savannah's business scene, it was inevitable we would do business with each other at some point. When your proposal came in, we had you investigated."

"Why?" But there was something Royce wanted to know more. "Actually, right now, I just want to know if my father has ever tried to do business with you."

Don nodded slowly. "He has attempted to work with us in the past. And, yes, I did investigate him just as thoroughly. But I didn't find the connection at that time."

He smiled at Royce. "I didn't need to investigate to see your relationship with Jasmine. It's all in her face, though she tries to hide it."

Royce could see it, too, every time she looked

at him. He was deeply worried his own feelings showed just as clearly, and he wasn't ready for that.

Don leaned back in his chair, causing it to creak. "As to why we investigate the personal backgrounds of potential business associates, I like to know who we're working with. Not just what you're capable of in a business arena, but who you are as a person. Unusual, but that's just how my wife and I like running our company. It works for us."

Royce wasn't sure how he felt about that. He could understand the concern, but the idea that his personal life had been scrutinized wasn't something he was comfortable acknowledging.

"Of course, we don't usually share that knowledge with our employees or contractors," Don said, "but in this instance, I felt it was particularly important."

"Again, why?"

"Well, I doubt this will make you feel any better about my snooping, but we happen to have taken a special interest in Jasmine Harden."

Royce wasn't above digging for his own information. This he wanted to hear. "My event planner?"

Don cocked his head to one side. "Is that all she is?"

"You tell me. You're the one hunting for info."

"Touché. You've just never been known to date much. She's never dated any of her clients."

This was getting more bizarre by the minute, but the fact that Don was concerned about Jasmine oddly reassured Royce. "I guess the real question is—is there a problem with anything you found out?" He might as well know if his history was about to stand in the way of his future.

"You've done very well for yourself—and in the best way possible. The only complaint I could find out about your company, or you for that matter, is that it isn't very child friendly."

"It's a business." *Not a day care.* But, for once, he kept that part to himself.

"I get that," Don conceded. "And a better understanding of a healthy work environment and happy employees will come to you with more life experience—but it's not a concern for us when it comes to doing business with you."

The proposal.

Don continued, "I'll be honest. I was skeptical at first. You see, we believe business should have a soul."

Royce shot his host a questioning look. The phrase sounded vaguely familiar. Royce wondered if it was something he'd read on Don's company website.

Luckily, Don was willing to enlighten him. "We believe that all of our business efforts should be done with our fellow man in mind wherever possible—helping take care of those who can't, keeping the environment stable and as unharmed by our work as possible, providing safe working conditions—and by extension, creating better living conditions for those who can't afford to do that for themselves."

Okay, this sounded familiar. The Jeffersons' company was known for its environmental stewardship and humanitarian working policies, in addition to its philanthropic efforts.

"When you first applied," Don continued, "I didn't believe this was a philosophy you readily embraced, despite your own efforts to make your shipping company as environmentally friendly as possible. Don't get me wrong—you've accomplished incredible things at a very young age."

Don grinned at Royce. "I can say that from my very advanced age and not sound Scroogy.

"Then I found out about your work with Jasmine. I know you have a charity event you are planning together. One we are much looking forward to, by the way. Sounds exciting."

Royce relaxed—a little. "Isn't anything Jasmine plans exciting?"

"Just about…" Don smiled. "She's an incredibly talented woman."

That was an understatement. Royce had learned more about the hidden depths of Jasmine Harden than he'd ever dreamed he would. She was smart, sexy, bold yet gracious, tenacious and amusing. And the first woman he'd ever wanted to stick around for longer than a night.

"My concern might sound a little old-fashioned. But I would never presume to insist that you marry her or stay with her. That's not anybody's place," Don conceded.

Royce acknowledged the sentiment with a nod.

"But she doesn't have a father present, and Marilyn and I are friends of hers, so I do feel a bit of a responsibility to request that you treat her decently. That's all any of us can expect."

"It's what any woman deserves," Royce said tightly, thinking of the man in the other room.

Don's nod was slow, almost contemplative. But Royce sensed it had nothing to do with studying him to get more inside information. Instead, the wisdom in Don's mature gaze told Royce he had more than an inkling about the hardships and poverty he'd suffered as a child...and why.

"I agree," Don finally said. "I'm glad to know we're on the same page."

Jasmine realized she was in for it when Marilyn smiled her way and asked, "So, Royce Brazier, huh?"

The older woman nodded sagely when Jasmine didn't answer right away. Instead she snagged them each a pretty mimosa off a passing waiter's tray. Jasmine sipped, grateful to have something to occupy her.

Under normal circumstances, she had no problem talking with Marilyn. They could cover a wide range of subjects without running out of steam. This time, she tried to act cool, but the blood rushed to her cheeks, anyway. She'd never discussed Royce like this outside of her family—and at home she was mainly deflecting her sisters' teasing.

His father standing across the room made her even more uncomfortable. She twisted the emerald ring round and round her finger until Marilyn laid a hand over hers. Jasmine met the older woman's understanding gaze.

"How did you know?" she asked.

Marilyn's expression showed delight that she'd guessed correctly. "I have a feeling about people. He isn't the first male client you've brought to our little get-togethers, but he's the first one you've looked at like that. Or who has looked at you the same way."

Suddenly Jasmine's mouth felt like a desert. She took a quick sip of the fizzy drink. "Like what?" she asked, almost afraid of the answer. So far, there'd been no one to see her with Royce except her sisters. And they were biased.

"Like he discovered a diamond in the midst of his sandbox. I remember." She leaned her head a little closer to confide, "Don looked at me that way, too."

"Really?"

Marilyn raised her glass. "I was his secretary," she said, then took a drink.

"No," Jasmine breathed. Somehow, she'd never thought to ask how Marilyn and Don had met. She'd just assumed Marilyn came from an upper-class family that wasn't from around here.

"Oh, yes, sweetheart. I married way above my class, which ended up being the scandal of the year. No one would mention it now, but they weren't afraid to criticize then. To Don's face, no less."

"I can't imagine." Jasmine felt privileged Marilyn was actually bringing up something this personal. "That must have been incredibly difficult."

"Don wasn't as powerful then—but he also wasn't as diplomatic. Or patient." Her smile was gracious, knowing. "People aren't quick to learn, you know. And Don doesn't enjoy repeating himself."

Jasmine doubted Royce would jeopardize his client relations to defend her like that, though she knew he wouldn't allow others to be disrespectful. She had no idea where his happy medium would be between the two stances—and had no desire to find out.

As if on cue, Royce's father appeared beside Marilyn. He wasn't as tall as his son, but their bearing was the same. Straight spine. Squared shoulders. Royce always looked as if he were bracing himself against whatever the world dared throw at him. His biological father looked like he knew what was coming and was prepared to take the hit. The gray creeping into his sandy hair reinforced the impression.

John Nave greeted them both but his eyes were trained on Jasmine. She shivered. Therein lay a key difference between the two men. Royce might be focused on his business, but his expression was still open. His father's was cold and closed down tight, not letting even a glimpse of emotion through. It was as if he evaluated her solely on what she was capable of providing him—and didn't care one bit about her as a person.

She'd never done business with Royce's father. And she hoped she never did.

One look at Marilyn and she knew her friend was aware of who he was—and possibly the story behind his connection to Royce. But Marilyn's smile as she turned to him was perfectly polite and diplomatic. "Mr. Nave, I'm surprised to see you here."

"These little get-togethers are good for business," he said, not bothering to look in Marilyn's direction. "Right, sweetheart?"

Shock shot through Jasmine. "Excuse me?"

"I said—"

"I heard what you said." Jasmine tightened the hand at her side into a fist, hoping it would help steady her...and her voice. "My name is Jasmine."

As if he didn't already know that. He nodded slowly, continuing to study her.

Jasmine glanced at her friend, who had let a frown break through her polite mask. Before she could say anything, John spoke again.

"There are also a lot of different kinds of distractions at these parties. Which are you?"

Okay, this was a bit much. She'd dealt with the public since she was a teenager and wasn't about to be walked all over—no matter who he was. She gifted them both with the sweetest smile she could muster. "I think distraction is good for you every now and again."

His eyebrow shot up, vaguely reminiscent of Royce when he was being obnoxious. "Not if you want to achieve success."

"Depends on the type of success you're aiming for," she countered.

"Very well put," Don said, as he and Royce joined them. Jasmine had been so focused on John that she hadn't noticed their approach. "I couldn't agree with you more, sweet Jasmine."

The endearment sounded so much nicer like that.

Don gave her a direct smile and an encouraging look. "I've always maintained that your intelligence is way above average—just like my dear Marilyn's."

Don stepped through the middle of their little gathering to gift his wife with a kiss. Jasmine was relieved to have a break from John's stare, though her tension was still through the roof.

"Darling, the caterer was looking for you," Don said. "Shall we?"

Marilyn nodded, smiling her goodbyes as Don settled her hand in the crook of his arm and led her away. Jasmine couldn't help but notice Marilyn didn't glance toward John. She was probably afraid she'd stick her tongue out at him.

Jasmine wanted to flip him the bird.

After the Jeffersons left them, Jasmine noticed that John had turned his stare toward his son. "I'm disappointed in you, Royce."

Heaven forbid we should make polite, pleasant conversation...

Royce wasn't daunted, though. He cocked his head to the side, looking down at the older man. "I'm not sure why you're bothering to think of me at all."

"As my only progeny, you'd be surprised how often you come to mind. Though I'm disappointed after our last meeting."

"Why?"

John shifted his gaze to Jasmine for only a moment. She could feel her thunderous emotions start to play out in her expression.

"I see you didn't take my advice."

"This is beginning to feel a little surreal," Royce said with a quick look around. "This conversation makes no sense whatsoever. Since when have I ever listened to anything you've said to me, on the rare occasions when you've said anything? Why would I start now?"

John shrugged, not seeming the least offended. "I've always hoped my genes would prevail."

"I believe the better genes did. My mother's."

Hear, hear.

"You can go so much farther, even farther than me, if you remain unattached. I mean, she's pretty," John said with a lazy gesture in Jasmine's direction. "And I'm not saying they aren't fun to play with…"

"Wow." Jasmine was amazed at the scene playing out in front of her…with her as the object of attention. Or, rather, derision. And she was done being a passive bystander. "Royce, let me say I agree with you. The better genes do prevail in you."

His father turned his hard gaze her way once more, but she wasn't backing down.

"It's a good thing your opinion doesn't count. At least, not for long."

Royce stepped forward, crowding into John's space. "Actually, her opinion counts for a whole lot more than yours—and it always will."

Fifteen

Anger pushed Royce to drive mindlessly. He sped out of the Jeffersons' long drive with a little more acceleration than was necessary. But the squeal of the tires on the asphalt gave him a brief moment of satisfaction.

He remained silent, teeth clenched, because if he spoke, the rage of years past might spew out on someone who didn't deserve it. So he locked himself down tight, his fists clenched around the wheel. His gaze was narrowed, focused solely on the road before him.

Only when they got to the parking garage of his building and he opened her car door did he tune in Jasmine. Her stillness. Her silence.

I'm not the only one involved.

He'd forgotten. It had been years since he'd had to worry about a woman's feelings, a woman's reactions. He remembered how his mother had internalized everything, taking the burden of whatever they'd endured onto herself as if she simply deserved it.

Jasmine certainly hadn't taken anything his father had dished out passively, though she'd maintained her ladylike demeanor better than his father had deserved. Now she sat looking up at him from the passenger seat, but she made no move to exit. Her posture was almost expectant, but his mind wasn't in a place to comprehend what she was waiting for.

"Something wrong?" he asked.

"I've been wondering if it was safe to ask you that."

As if realizing he was losing patience, she got out of the car but lagged behind as he strode toward the elevator.

"What?" He winced when his voice echoed off the brick and concrete walls of the garage, and he heard just how impatient he sounded.

"Do you really want me here?" she asked.

Her confusion and the lost note in her voice were finally breaking through his self-absorption. He softened his tone. "Unless you don't want to be here. I can't stop you from leaving, Jasmine."

"You already have."

Royce glanced around in confusion. "What?"

"My car isn't here," she pointed out, exaggerating her enunciation, probably hoping he'd catch on.

That's when he remembered picking her up at her house. He squeezed his eyes closed and cursed under his breath. How had he let that man get so far under his skin?

Jasmine.

Royce opened his eyes and looked at her expression, which was now slightly amused. Though he could still detect some concern lingering around the edges.

This was why he'd gotten so upset. So angry.

Royce had become immune to his father's reprimands and insults throughout the years, though his conversations with his father were few and far between.

Just the way he liked it.

So this anger wasn't about him. More than anything, Royce didn't want Jasmine hurt by his father. He didn't even want her touched by anything his father said or did.

Now he understood why his mom hadn't fought very hard. It wasn't like she'd had a lot of options. Certainly no lawyer in town had been willing to let her set foot in their firm.

Officially, it had always been her word against his father's. Those close to the situation had known the truth. But his mother simply hadn't wanted to be in the same room with the man who could treat her so disrespectfully after she'd served her purpose. The man who would threaten her and her son so he didn't have to part with the paltry sum it would have taken to lift their lives above poverty level.

Better to cut that person from her life than to allow him to destroy her, piece by piece, over years of contact.

That hadn't been an option for Royce, if he wanted to be any kind of businessman in Savannah. But he'd done his best to ignore John over the years. John seemed to prefer it that way, too.

Now it seemed his father had taken some kind of interest in him.

Royce refused to let that dictate anything about who he was or his actions.

Reaching out, he took Jasmine's hand in his. But he just stood there. He didn't rush upstairs. Instead, he let his eyes close once more and let the early summer breeze carry her scent to him. When he opened his eyes and his gaze found her face, he took in how she was patiently waiting. He offered a sheepish smile.

"Would you like to come up for a while?"

"Only if that's where you want me."

Silly woman. "I can't think of anything I want more right now."

"Me, either."

That's when he noticed the slight strain in her smile, the tightness around her eyes. Their encounter with his father had affected her almost as much as it had him.

But he waited until much later, when he held her tight against him in his bed, to ask, "What did he say to you before I showed up?"

The delicious lassitude that fitted her perfectly to his side drained away. He felt her body stiffen, though she didn't retreat from him. "Honestly, I'm doing my best to forget. Let's just say, your dad is very much a sexist pig."

"First of all, he isn't my dad. He's the sperm donor."

His tone was light, and sure enough, she laughed. Unfortunately, the sentiment came straight from his heart.

"Second of all, it amazes me how he knew anyone willing to bring him. As you can tell, he isn't the most personable of people. But money talks."

"It must, because I can't imagine how that man ever got married." A shiver shook her body.

Royce hugged her closer. "I agree. Although, from the rumors I've heard, she's just as cold."

"Then why bother? I don't understand."

Neither did Royce. "It's marriage as a business merger. They're the perfect example."

"An example of what not to do," Jasmine murmured.

"I guess it works for them." He shrugged. "I'd rather be alone than endure something that emotionless."

She patted his chest. "That's because you actually have a heart...and human emotions."

"I know a few people who wouldn't agree with you," he said with a chuckle.

"*I* might not have agreed with me a month ago."

"And I wouldn't blame you for your assessment."

She snuggled closer. Her breath was warm across his skin. She was silent for so long that he began to wonder if she'd fallen asleep. Then she whispered, "So why be that way?"

It's safe. There was no way he was offering that explanation. Not even to Jasmine. Instead, he said, "It's what I know."

"What do I wear to the ball? Cinderella's eternal question shared by women everywhere."

Jasmine glared at her little sister as she walked past, her arms overflowing with formal dresses. Ivy's words made Jasmine even more stressed. The store owner helped Ivy arrange her potential choices on a rack before she headed down the hall to a dressing room. Jasmine's arms were still empty.

They'd been looking at dresses for the masquerade for over half an hour already at a small local boutique where Jasmine usually bought her formal clothing. Ivy was attending the masquerade with her. She loved parties. Willow was more than happy to help pick out everyone's attire, then stay home with Auntie and Rosie.

The three of them had done this on quite a few occasions. Many times Ivy had assisted Jasmine at her events so she had an extra pair of hands. This time, her little sister was coming because what Jasmine and Royce had put together was totally cool.

But Jasmine had never had a problem finding a dress. Today was the exception, apparently.

She knew what the problem was, but she didn't want to acknowledge it. What difference did it make what dress she wore? After all, Royce had seen her naked on more than one occasion. But her stupid feminine psyche seemed stuck on finding *the perfect* dress. The dress that would wow Royce, make him proud to have her standing next to him.

At least, she assumed that's what she would be doing…when she wasn't conferring with caterers and waitstaff and Dominic, among others. Royce hadn't actually spelled that part out yet.

But she wasn't going to live with the same angst she'd had before their visit to the Jeffersons' Sunday Salon. They'd gone out to dinner a few times since then. She'd felt safe assuming they'd present themselves as a couple, of sorts. By now she knew Royce wasn't the type of man who needed her on his arm the entire time. But when they were together, she knew he wouldn't ignore her.

Still, she hoped she got to have at least one dance with him...

"So, what's the problem?" Willow asked.

"I just can't find what I'm looking for." Jasmine glanced once more across the rows and rows of silky fabrics and sequins.

"What *are* you looking for?" Willow asked, the confusion in her voice echoing Jasmine's own conflicted emotions.

"I haven't figured that out, either."

Luckily, Willow didn't lose patience quickly. "At least we know where the problem is."

Jasmine tried to explain. "I don't want it to be

too sexy, because I'm also there in a professional capacity. But I also don't want it to be too businesslike, because…"

"Royce won't find that sexy?"

It took her a minute to admit it. "Well, yes."

"Where are these nerves still coming from? Y'all are great together."

And Jasmine knew that was true. In every single way except one: Rosie. After seeing Royce with his father, she knew better than anyone why he limited his time around children. A conviction that deep wasn't going to disappear overnight. She felt like she had to protect at least part of her heart, when what she really wanted was to jump in with both feet and leave her worries in the dust.

"I really enjoy being with Royce," she began.

Ivy stuck her head out of her dressing room. "Of course you do."

"But I just don't know that it can ever be something permanent."

Willow seemed to get this, although Ivy rolled her eyes. "Don't you trust Royce?" Ivy asked.

"In just about every way."

Willow peeked at her solemnly over the stack

of dresses she'd started loading into her arms. "Then what is it that's holding you back?"

"Rosie."

"Why?" Ivy asked again.

"Babies are a big responsibility."

Ivy shrugged. "He seems to do fine whenever he's with her."

"But the occasional cuddle here and there isn't the same as living with a child. Royce has...issues."

"This is true," Willow confirmed.

Ivy, however, wasn't convinced. "What kind of issues?"

Jasmine forced herself back to her task, listlessly sifting through the racks. She wasn't sharing Royce's secrets. They were his to share, not hers. Willow reached over her to pick up dresses she'd overlooked.

After an uninspired search, they wandered toward the dressing rooms with just a few items. "Did the Jeffersons give you flack because you're dating your client?" Willow asked.

"Nope. Which surprised me a little. I wasn't sure how they'd feel." Jasmine glanced over at Willow and lowered her voice a little, even though they were the only ones there at the moment. "Turns out Marilyn used to be Don's secretary."

Willow's green eyes went wide. "Wow. Never would have guessed that one. Every time I've met them, she just seems to...fit."

"I know. From admin assistant to billionaire wife. She has always seemed the perfect person to be at Don's side."

Ivy called from her dressing room. "Ooh, maybe I should join the trend..."

Jasmine was standing in the hallway not far from Ivy's curtained alcove. "It isn't as easy as you think."

"Why not?"

Jasmine couldn't tell if Ivy was being serious or just giving her older sister a hard time, which she liked to do on occasion.

"What if it ends?" Jasmine finally asked. "You're in the position of needing a new job then. If just one of you decides it isn't working, it can get messy. How do you act in front of people?" Jasmine was up close and personal with that particular situation, which was made even trickier because her business was dependent on appearances. "How much do you tell? How much do you keep to yourself? It's just very complicated."

"True. Still…"

Willow leaned closer but didn't bother to lower her voice. "Have you seen Ivy's boss? He's dreamy. He might actually be worth the risk."

"Well, if Ivy thinks it's worth it, *she* can have this ring." It was just complicating Jasmine's life. Though she'd never admit it to her sisters, the ring had indeed done its job. She couldn't deny that she wanted Royce forever…but a big part of her still doubted she would actually have him that long.

"Maybe the night of the masquerade," Ivy said, "especially if I wear this—"

She came out of the dressing room in a formal green dress. It faithfully followed her curves. Jewel chips formed flowers across the bodice and down one hip. The fit was gorgeous on Ivy's petite yet rounded figure. The color perfectly complemented her dark blond hair.

"Wow, Ivy," Jasmine breathed. "That's beautiful."

"Considering he's never seen me in anything but a business suit, I certainly hope *my* boss thinks so..."

Sixteen

Jasmine hung her dress in the alcove off the ballroom of Keller House, once again amazed at its brilliant blue color. The off-the-shoulder style and intricate beading were perfect. A fitted bodice flowed into a layered, full skirt that showcased her shape. Thank goodness the owner of the shop had stepped in and found an answer to her dress conundrum.

If only everything else were that easy.

The next two days certainly wouldn't be. She was at Keller House today to oversee the final setup. Most of tomorrow would be spent in preparation for the masquerade tomorrow night, and then there would be the event itself. Sunday she was hoping for a lazy sleep in, but as little as poor Rosie had seen of her this week, she wasn't holding her breath that the munchkin would co-operate.

She could at least have a lazy Sunday at home, though.

She made her way through the finished hall-ways to the incredible kitchen Royce had had installed. It was up and running, the catering staff currently finding a home for everything. She could see Geraldine laying out her plan and giving instructions on how to execute it. Having worked with the woman before, Jasmine didn't think there would be any problems there. Geral-dine was as thorough and organized as Jasmine.

It would all work. The food was one area Jas-mine didn't have to worry a lot about, but she couldn't stop herself from going over her check-list.

"Dominic, are you bumming samples?" Jas-mine teased when she found the photographer in the kitchen.

He grinned. "Busted."

"We can always use an independent taste test," Geraldine said.

"Then you are a more generous woman than me." Jasmine smiled. "Of course, I know exactly how much he likes the sweet stuff. Doesn't Greg keep you in good supply at home?"

"Don't give away my secrets," Dominic said in a mock whisper.

"Okay...I'll distract you with a video, instead."

"Miss Rosie?" he asked.

"You bet."

Jasmine pulled out her phone and cued up the video Ivy had sent her from the night before. She'd been in the other room on the phone, confirming the catering list. Her sisters hadn't wanted to yell and distract Rosie, so they'd videoed it while they could. Thank goodness for modern digital technology.

Dominic gasped when Rosie started to show off her new crawling skills. "She's been rocking for a couple of weeks now..." Jasmine explained.

"And she just took off?"

Jasmine nodded. The excited conversation attracted the attention of the caterer and the kitchen staff, who converged on the phone to see Jasmine's daughter's new and exciting prowess.

Dominic shook his head, eyeing Jasmine with a mischievous look over the crowd. "Oh, you are in trouble now, girl."

"For what?" Royce asked as he entered the room. His business voice was one she rarely heard anymore—the no-nonsense, almost stern tone he used to command and commandeer. She and the entire kitchen staff jumped.

Dominic ignored them. "Check out this video of Rosie, Royce."

Jasmine suddenly felt like a kid caught with her hand in the cookie jar. The phrase *not a day care* roamed round and round in her brain. Not only had she been discussing her daughter in detail during work hours, but she'd distracted the staff with the video, also.

She was disrupting their productivity and focus...

Surprisingly, Royce did look at the video...actually, he frowned. To Jasmine's shock, he then swiped a finger across the phone and started the video over again.

Finally, he said, "She crawled? Even though she's so little?"

Royce's gaze met hers, and she could see her own feelings mirrored in his eyes. Awe, excitement and a touch of fear.

Dominic said, "Cool, isn't it?"

"She's actually crawling right on time," Jasmine said, unable to quell her need to chatter. "Seven months. The doctors had worried about issues with her motor skills after..." Jasmine swallowed hard, trying to push back the memories of Rosie's mother struggling with drugs early in her pregnancy to ease the pain of her cancer. But the moment she'd known Rosie was there, she'd never touched anything her doctor didn't approve. "But she's a little trouper."

Royce shook his head slowly back and forth. "I'd be afraid of stepping on her or losing her."

Jasmine and Dominic shared a smile. "Well, it's not like I'm suddenly giving her free rein in the neighborhood or the keys to the car," Jasmine teased.

Dominic nodded in her direction. "Trust me, it's time to invest in some baby gates. She'll be into everything, as curious as she is."

"How do you know?" Royce asked.

Dominic puffed his chest out. "Proud, loving uncle to five nieces and nephews."

"Five?" Royce's surprise amused Jasmine.

"That's right," Dominic confirmed. "Five. And this little cutie is gonna be a handful. I guarantee it."

"I'd rather you didn't," Jasmine warned.

Despite her concern, Jasmine felt the glow of maternal pride. It was still fairly new, though less tentative than when Rosie had been a newborn. It had taken a while to give herself permission to feel it, to embrace it. Even though she'd legally been Rosie's mother from day one, it had taken time for her to grow into the role. She'd shared the daily responsibilities with Rosie's biological mother until she hadn't been able to help anymore. Her health had gone downhill rapidly after Rosie's birth. Her death had thrown Jasmine headlong into the reality of being responsible for such a small being's life.

Dominic winked. "Oh, before you know it, she'll be standing beside you at events like this in her own ball gowns."

Jasmine was shaking her head before he even

finished, the words causing a distant panic to mix in with her pride. "Let's get through the challenges of potty training first...for now, back to work."

More than anything, she didn't want to push her luck with Royce. He'd been pretty understanding about this whole thing, had even participated in the conversation, but she was holding up progress here. Any minute he might remember that.

With a quick wave and a chorus of goodbyes from the kitchen staff, Jasmine headed back down the hallway to check out the formal living area where they were setting up carnival-type booths. Albeit for a very fancy carnival, that was for sure. Royce suddenly appeared at her side. For several moments, Jasmine maintained their silence.

She could tell Royce wanted to ask her something. She was simply afraid of what it was.

"Why weren't you there?" he finally asked.

"Where?"

"Watching Rosie crawl."

Jasmine froze, feeling as if someone had just

punched the air from her lungs. She took a deep, extra-heavy breath, then said, "I was in the other room, confirming the menu with Marco."

She could feel her body stiffening, bracing herself for his derision.

"I'm sorry," he said simply.

What? "No *I told you so*?" Even though she kept her tone mild, Jasmine knew the words weren't. But frankly, she was tired of playing a guessing game. Now was as good a time as any to figure out where Royce stood on the subject of her and her child.

Even if it might burst her romantic bubble.

To her surprise, Royce reached out to rub his thumb across her left cheekbone. "My mother would say you've given me a wonderful gift."

His soft tone, his happy expression, reduced her question to a whisper. "What's that?"

"Helping me to see that women do whatever is necessary...which isn't always the same as what they want."

For a moment, Jasmine held her breath, afraid she might cry.

"What is it?" Royce finally asked.

"Your words are a gift to me, too."

* * *

Later that evening, everyone but Jasmine had finally left the restored mansion. She could almost feel the emptiness as she made one last check of the areas of the second floor that would be open to the public at tomorrow's masquerade.

In midafternoon, Royce had finally left to take care of some things at his office. Dominic had finalized the process for photographs and finished setting up the incredible photo booth. The backdrop was a doctored photograph of the house itself, looking mysterious draped in gray fog under a full moon struggling to be seen. Guests would sit in an elegant open carriage polished to a fine shine. Even Jasmine couldn't wait to have her picture taken.

She'd made the last touches to the flower arrangements on the side tables and in the seating areas. The ice sculpture would be delivered tomorrow, along with the centerpieces for the dining tables.

On her way back to the ballroom, Jasmine checked the long parlor along the front of the house where the carnival booths were set up. The whole length of the house had been beautifully restored, lovingly repainted with gold leaf accents. The chandeliers were original crystal period pieces and the long parlor had vintage wallpaper that Royce's contractor had ordered from overseas. But there was only one place in the house that caused Jasmine to hold her breath when she stepped in: the ballroom.

It was hard to believe people had homes with literal ballrooms in them anymore. But Royce's made Jasmine feel like a princess whenever she walked over the threshold. One entire side featured a series of large mirrors hanging in gilded frames. The rest of the walls had panels of hand-painted murals of lords and ladies from centuries past. Jasmine had only seen them in a horrible, degraded state. The experts Royce had brought in had restored them to their former glory as closely as possible.

Jasmine walked across the refinished floors, the click of her heels echoing. She went directly to the far wall where there was a hidden door in one of the panels. With a simple push, it allowed entrance to an alcove, but getting the right spot without knowing it beforehand was almost impossible. The room might once have been a ladies' sitting room, a place for women to catch their breath on elegant chaises, fix their hair and check makeup in the mirror of the old-fashioned vanity, or simply stare out the window over the back gardens.

Jasmine had a sudden itch to see her dress in the ballroom mirrors before tomorrow night's crowd cluttered the view. After stripping to her underwear, she took the gown carefully down off the hanger and stepped into it.

Only half of the chandeliers were on in the ballroom, giving it an even more magical feel. Jasmine had kept her heels on, so only the barest hint of the bottom edge of her dress touched the floor. Once, twice, she absently twirled before the mirrors.

The lights sparkled off the bodice and the tiny jewels adorning the edges of each layer of the skirt. Definitely princess material. She couldn't quite bring herself to pretend she was dancing, but the skirt flared out elegantly as she turned around and around in a circle. On one twirl, she spotted a shape in the doorway. Her heart jumped, throat closing for a moment until Royce stepped out into the soft light. Her pause was involuntary. It was as if everything stilled, waiting for him to lead the dance they'd come to share.

Royce walked slowly toward her, the look in his eyes nowhere close to businesslike. He was wearing his everyday suit, not a tux, but he pulled off a princely demeanor, anyway.

Feeling the pressure to fill the silence, she said, "Your mother would love what you've accomplished here. This house is magnificent."

He kept his solemn expression as he moved closer to her. "She'd appreciate it far more than my business accomplishments. I'm sure you would agree."

"Actually, Royce, I'm a businesswoman myself. While I love what you've done with the place in your mother's honor, I realize you couldn't create something this incredible without being successful in your professional life."

"She didn't approve of my work in many ways, didn't want me to follow my father's path."

Which he'd done wholeheartedly...until now. "But you haven't really, have you? You aren't your father."

He nodded slowly, as if he were thinking over his answer. "Maybe not."

Finally he stood before her, studying her with dramatic effect before stepping close to take her into his arms. But before he moved, he used one crooked finger to lift her chin so she could meet his look.

"Jasmine, I'll be so proud to have you by my side tomorrow."

Then he started to dance her around the room. There was no music, just the rhythm created by his body. Several times Jasmine caught the surreal sight of them in one of the mirrors. An elegant man and lady moving in time with each other. The fabric of her brilliant blue dress swirled and brushed over the legs of his pants.

But it was the look in his eyes that held her enthralled.

She'd been through so many changes this year. She'd lost a friend. She'd gained a child. She'd embarked on a journey as a mother. But, for the first time in a long time, her doubts were quiet and she was completely happy.

Maybe he will *accept all of me.*

Seventeen

Royce couldn't quite believe the woman in his arms was his. Soft. Sweet, with just enough spice. And he had no doubt that she was giving herself to him fully in this moment.

Was it possible to feel humbled and powerful at the same time?

He'd certainly never had the heady experience before, but he wasn't going to waste it. With the expert skill he'd never thought he'd need, he waltzed Jasmine in a full circle around the room, coming to rest near the alcove door. Knowing the house had been cleared of workers, he didn't bother leading her to a more secluded spot.

Privacy wasn't as important as their hunger for each other.

He thanked the universe for the opportunity and crowded her against the wall with his body. Her eyes widened. Her breasts plumped above the edge of her dress. Her skin was pale against the deep blue. Royce wanted to explore every inch, but for tonight, he would taste her right here.

His lips stroked over hers. He savored the mewling from her throat as their tongues entwined. She tasted of surrender, though he knew her strength; she had tested him with it more than once. And would again in the future.

But, for tonight, she was his.

She wasn't a passive princess. Her deft fingers unbuttoned his jacket then slid inside to spread warmth to his ribs through his thin dress shirt. Her touch sent a surge of need rushing through him. His hips pressed closer. She gasped.

He had to taste more of her.

Bending low, he placed his mouth right below her ear. One of the most tempting things Jasmine did to him every day was wear her hair up. It was gorgeous down, and it was pure pleasure burying his hands in its thickness. But when it was pulled up into a twist, a bun or, hell, even a ponytail, he couldn't resist the length of her neck and the sensitive skin he knew was there.

She clutched at him once more as his mouth covered the pulse point below her ear. Her breath hitched as he suckled lightly. The tension invading her body drove his own need higher. The fact that he knew how to make this woman ache with pleasure brought him the most satisfaction of anything he'd experienced thus far in life.

It was addictive. Necessary.

Slowly, he let himself meander the familiar but exciting path down her straining muscles. Her skin was smooth. Her body was responsive on every level. He lapped at the hollow at the base of her throat, savoring the rapid beat of her pulse. Her cries filled his ears. He knew without a doubt that she was ready for him.

But he wasn't taking things any further without sampling the top curve of her breasts, slightly salty from her day of work. He pulled her closer and lifted her higher with his hands at her waist. The tender flesh plumped beneath his lips. He couldn't stop working her until he nuzzled one tight nipple. Her textures and flavors amazed him.

He drew on her carefully, knowing how sensitive she was here. Her cries grew loud enough to echo off the walls. Strange how satisfying that was to hear. Royce played for long moments, feeling her fists clench and pull at his shirt.

Now. He needed her now.

With more haste than finesse, he scrambled beneath the layers at the front of her dress until his hands found skin. Then he followed the trembling muscles of her thighs to her damp underwear. Quickly he stripped it from her.

Mine. Mine.

He readied himself, practically tearing open his fly and fitting on a condom. He lifted one of her legs, making a place for himself between them. The moment that he slid inside, her head fell back against the wall. He captured her open mouth as he forged into her. The thrust and retreat was exquisite. His hips drove hard as she gasped out his name.

The feelings were too intense to last long. In a flash, they were both consumed. He gave one last thrust and her body clamped down on his with a demand of her own. And he obeyed without protest.

In the throbbing, heated aftermath, Royce knew a part of himself was now forever tied to this woman. For the first time, he could admit that he had no desire to fight the pull.

Jasmine's heart thrilled at the sight of hundreds of masked attendees in line to enter the mansion. The dark tuxes and formal gowns befit the setting, taking her back to a bygone era when this house was a mecca for Savannah society. The masks ranged from plain and simple to elegant affairs adorned with sparkles and feathers. They lent just the right touch of mystery, even when Jasmine knew who the wearer was.

Excitement filled the air as guests made their way inside. The chatter of each group transformed into oohs and aahs as they discovered all the wonderful entertainments available in the various rooms.

After most of the guests had arrived, Jasmine turned to the next person in line, only to discover Francis Staten. His long hair had had a slight trim and he sported a smooth new tux. She smiled. "Well, don't you look spiffy?"

His grin was a little shame-faced. "I was just gonna dust off the old suit, but Royce had this delivered. I feel almost guilty wearing it."

"Don't." After years of seeing him in his khakis at the mission, she completely understood. Still... "Let him do this for you. Represent the mission tonight, in the midst of these people, with pride in all you do every day."

Jasmine knew how much more confident and comfortable she was among Savannah's elite when she dressed the part.

"I don't want people to think—"

"No, Francis. No one will think you are using the mission's money to buy yourself a suit. If they do, they won't understand what we're trying to do there, anyway. Just enjoy yourself, have a glass of champagne and talk us up."

"At least I'm comfortable giving speeches. Unlike wearing this bow tie."

He pulled at his collar as he walked away, but Jasmine was glad to see him join a conversation almost immediately. She didn't want him to feel alone all evening. Royce paused for a few moments to greet Francis, then made his way back to Jasmine's side.

His black tux and matching half mask set off his blond hair. Jasmine could have watched him walk toward her all day. He was so incredibly sexy…and all hers.

"Everything is going very well," he said, as he bent to kiss her.

"Thank you," she murmured against his lips.

He pulled back a fraction. "For what?"

"Francis's tux," she said, nodding in the other man's direction.

Royce glanced over his shoulder before turning back to her. "I figured it would help him feel more comfortable here. If he had the money for one, that's certainly not what he would spend it on."

"How did you know that?" Because Royce was exactly right.

His dark gaze was intense behind the mask. "I know a few things about people, you know. Even if I've never put them to good use in social situations before."

"Well, thank you for seeing that."

"Thank you for taking me to the mission so I could see it."

Before Jasmine had a chance to savor his words, the Jeffersons appeared before them. "Jasmine," Don said, "you have gone above and beyond this time. This masquerade is incredible."

Marilyn Jefferson's eyes sparkled behind her purple feathered mask. "And this house! I didn't even realize it was being renovated."

"For several years now," Royce said. "In honor of my mother. She loved this place."

"I'm sure," Marilyn said with a soft smile. "I just hate that she didn't see it like this. In the glory you've worked so hard to achieve."

Jasmine explained, "She lived in the carriage house for a few years as the renovations began."

"The final version that I executed is almost identical to the plans she drew up herself," Royce said.

"Congratulations, Royce," Don said. "Tonight will be a smashing success, I know. For you and the mission. On Monday, let's make an appointment. To talk."

Jasmine knew Royce wanted to smile big,

but he kept it under wraps pretty well. Still, she could feel the jolt of excitement that ran through his body. "I will set that up. Thank you, sir."

After the Jeffersons had walked away, Jasmine kissed Royce hard and long, not caring who watched. "Congratulations," she finally murmured.

The evening was as successful as Don Jefferson had predicted. Preliminary counts said they had earned more than enough money to pay for a nice, large building with sleeping quarters on the mission's campus and some additional upgrades, as well.

It wasn't until after the big announcements late in the evening that Jasmine even realized Royce's father was there.

She recognized that analytical gaze easily, despite the plain black mask he sported. Just the feel of him looking in her direction made her stomach clench and bile back up in her throat. Yet, for the next half hour, she saw him everywhere she looked, no matter what she was doing.

Finally she was able to break away from her hostessing duties and find Royce. To warn him. But she arrived only seconds before his father did.

Royce glared at the man over her shoulder. "You're not welcome here."

Jasmine turned to find John completely unmoved by Royce's anger.

"I bought a ticket," he said with a shrug.

"And I'll happily refund your money."

John cocked his head to the side, studying Royce as if to figure out exactly what he needed to say to get through to the man before him. "If word got around that you threw me out, that might hurt donations."

"We don't need any more." Royce's expression was undeniably proud. "But if we did, I'd make it up out of my own pocket."

"That's not good business, Royce. You know that." John shook his head as if Royce were behaving childishly. "You cannot let your emotions rule over money."

"Tonight's not about business," Jasmine insisted.

But the look John turned her way reminded her she wasn't speaking for herself. "You sure?"

Suddenly she remembered Don Jefferson's invitation to set up an appointment with Royce. The real reason he had started this venture so long ago. But before she could respond, Ivy appeared at her elbow. "Jasmine, the catering lady has a question. She's looking for you."

"Right," John said, "Go on back to work now."

Royce stepped firmly between her and his father, brushing a brief kiss over her brow. "Go ahead," he murmured. "Don't worry. I'll handle dear old Dad."

Eighteen

So Jasmine left, but forty-five minutes later, she realized that Royce was nowhere to be found. Oh, the party was in full swing without him, but that didn't defuse the worry that settled in her gut.

She knew he wasn't in the front parlor, because she'd just been through there. Everything was running smoothly and the vendors had given her very positive feedback. But there'd been no sign of Royce.

Next, she checked the ballroom as best as she could. Between the dancers and those milling around listening to the small orchestra, it was a little too crowded for an accurate reading. But she didn't see him. The kitchen and dining rooms were also a bust.

Though he could have stepped outside to cool off, that didn't feel right. Besides, Jasmine wasn't familiar enough with the grounds to trust herself to go looking around in the dark.

Instead, she climbed the back stairs. Several rooms at the front of the second floor had been opened for guests to tour, including a grand sitting room and a couple of bedrooms. There were other completed rooms on this floor that weren't open for viewing. One she knew to be an office that Royce had set up with equipment in case he needed to be reached or do something while he was out here—which he often had been during the last month or so.

As she reached the top of the stairs, muffled voices reached her. Alert that there was someone in the office, she approached the closed door with trepidation. Why would Royce have brought his father up here? Or was it just someone else he'd wanted to talk to?

She didn't want to interrupt business. But the

thought that he would be taking a business meeting in the middle of their event was upsetting.

At first she thought the door was closed, but as she reached it, she realized it was cracked. The voices filtered through enough that she recognized Royce...and his father. She should have just turned away, gone back downstairs and left Royce to handle it. Instead, she reached out and pushed the door back an inch, allowing her to see a small sliver of the scene inside.

John Nave flicked a silver lighter, then used it to light a thin cigar. He puffed a few times, causing the tip to glow red. "I, more than anyone, know how disruptive women can be," he finally said.

Royce turned to him. The lamp nearby allowed Jasmine to read the surprise on his face. Unconcerned, his father blew out a stream of cigar smoke. "Yes, your mother wasn't the first. But she was the only one I made the mistake of getting pregnant."

"I wouldn't consider myself a mistake."

John paused in that way he had, as if he considered every word before speaking it. "I did, at the time. But I've checked in through the years.

You've turned out well. Still, I felt it was best if I married after that."

Royce scoffed. "I wouldn't call what you have a marriage. More like a business arrangement."

"I call it the best of both worlds. I handle the business. She handles the house and our image. And takes the edge off when I really need it. What more could I want?"

Jasmine waited for Royce to say *love*, but he remained silent.

"You've made a terrible misstep, son. I've seen the way you look at her. You're going soft. Besides, that woman has a baby, for Christ's sake. One that's not even hers."

"How did you find that out?" Royce stalked closer to stand over John's chair. "Never mind. I'm sure I can guess. A better question is, why do you care?"

"Because *you* should," John insisted, gaining his feet to meet Royce head-on. "You should care that her middle-class family is going to suck your focus away from your business. Why would you let someone like that stand in the way of achieving all that you can?"

Royce's voice hardened. "I have never let anything stand in the way of my success. I'm not about to start now."

John extended his hand to shake Royce's. "Good. I'm glad to hear that."

Jasmine's last look showed Royce and his father standing close to each other, hands clasped, the picture of power and business acumen.

There was no place in that picture for family or all the tender, passionate emotions Royce inspired inside her. Emotions he obviously didn't return. Had he been pretending all along?

Turning, Jasmine fled back along the hall and down the staircase, holding her quiet sobs inside and lifting her skirt just enough to keep her from tripping and breaking a bone.

She rushed along the hall behind the kitchen, her only thought that she needed out before she broke down completely. Then she ran smack into someone tall and solid.

"Sugar, what's the matter?" Dominic asked.

Just hearing his voice brought reality back in a rush. Jasmine clutched at the front of his jacket, dragging in deep breaths in an attempt to get herself under control. Unfortunately, that just made the darkened hall whirl around her. "I feel dizzy."

"Come here."

Dominic clutched her to his solid chest as he led her to a small storage room where he pulled out one of the folding chairs they were using for seating in the dining room and settled her into it. Then he opened one for himself and sat next to her.

"Now, tell me what's wrong."

Jasmine shook her head, unable to put into words the pain she felt. "I trusted him."

"Who?" Dominic asked, laying his large hand against the bare skin of her upper back. His heat calmed her, centered her focus on that one spot. Oddly enough, it made her realize that the rest of her body was chilled, inside and out.

"Royce. I thought…" Why had she thought that she would be enough to make the leopard change his spots? "I thought maybe he might be different."

"Was he ugly to you? Did he hurt you?"

"No." *He simply chose business over me.* "I just overheard something I shouldn't have."

"Maybe you didn't hear enough."

She hadn't wanted to hear more. She shook her head. "I don't know if I can do this."

Dominic's hand flexed against her, drawing her focus away from the pain in her heart. "You can," he said. "Tonight is your crowning glory, and it's almost over. Ivy and I will help you finish what you need to, I promise."

Jasmine just hoped that would be enough.

Royce concentrated hard on the feel of John's hand against his, letting the sounds of the party in the house disappear. He'd never touched his father before. He'd never wanted to be this close to him.

Just as he'd expected, the grip was firmer than it needed to be—a competition to see who could outman the other. It wasn't the recognition and respect Royce had exchanged with men like Don Jefferson. Men who were high achievers in their businesses, but who were also intent on contributing to the greater good in their families, their communities and the world.

Royce tightened his hold before stepping in, mere inches away from his father. He had to admit the slight advantage he had in height made him feel superior, even though it was a petty sentiment that shouldn't have a place here. Then again, his father preferred for this meeting to be about strength, and probably his own superiority to his son. Apparently, he'd come here to school Royce in how he should live.

But he had no lessons Royce needed to learn.

He found himself leaning close to his father's face, looking him dead in the eye and acknowledging the biological link between the two of them. Then he grinned, because he didn't have to base his life and decisions on that biology. Or, rather, he'd prefer his maternal biology to any genes this man had passed on to him.

"That's right," he said, his voice low but clear. "I've never let anything stand in the way of achieving my goals…only my goals have changed."

John's eyes widened as Royce's grip turned punishing. After a few seconds, Royce turned away. But he wasn't done proving his point. "Success isn't defined by money, *Father*, despite this belief system that you've built your life upon. I've seen many examples in the business community of men who care just as much about their fellow man as they do about themselves."

"And they're poorer because of it," John insisted.

"How much money do you really need to live, John? After all, you can only drive one Rolls Royce at a time."

The other man's gaze flared at Royce's words.

"I'd rather have one or two fewer cars and build a dormitory for homeless men at the City Sanctuary mission. I'd rather make a little less money on a shipping contract and know that people are getting life-saving supplies that they need. After all, I only require one place to live."

He gestured around the luxury office he'd built here at Keller House. "All of this is simply surplus."

Royce returned to his post behind the large mahogany desk but didn't sit down. Instead, he faced his father—businessman to businessman. "But most important, John, I'd rather have the love of a good woman and a family as my legacy than the money to build a huge mausoleum for all the people who couldn't give a rat's ass about visiting my grave after I'm gone. That's *my* definition of success."

"You're wrong."

"Am I? Because tonight I have my money, my woman and a child with the sweetest smile in the world. A child who deserves a chance to achieve her own success, no matter who contributed to her biological makeup. What do you have besides your money, a wife who couldn't care less about you and a big, empty house?"

Royce braced his hands on the desktop, staring the other man down. "Now, while this little family reunion has been very enlightening, in the future, you will not contact me. If you see me in public, you will walk the other way. If you see my future wife, future child, employees or anyone associated with me, you will keep on walking. If you don't, I will make sure you regret it. Because I don't need you in my life."

It was almost amusing to see his father draw his body straighter, even though he was facing defeat. "I doubt you can do that."

"Oh, I can. You see, I know what you value the most, *Father*. And while I'm sure you had plenty of cronies to help you disavow me and leave my mother poverty-stricken while she raised your child, this is a new day. A new culture. And news of the steps you took to ruin that woman and your biological child won't go over nearly as well in today's business climate—especially coming straight from that child himself. Who is now a very successful man in his own right."

Royce smiled, though he knew it wasn't a pleasant expression. "So I will warn you again— you keep your mouth shut. That is, if you want me to do the same."

Nineteen

Jasmine kept herself busy. Since she knew she would need to leave sooner rather than later, she quietly made preparations to disappear once the midnight unveiling had happened. For the first time ever, she had no plans to stay at her event until the last guest had left and the last plate was packed.

Ivy seemed to have disappeared while Jasmine was upstairs, and she wasn't answering her phone, so Jasmine went to the point person in each area to make sure they were covered. Plans had been made to close the party at 2:00 a.m. Every staff member knew what was expected of them. A cleaning crew would be here tomorrow.

She'd hoped her sister would stay behind as her eyes and ears, but she'd make do as best she could. Who knew how long she'd be able to hold all these emotions inside? And the last thing she wanted was to make small talk with Royce while wondering if he was simply humoring her to get her into bed.

There was nothing she wanted more than to get out of this dress and be home with her family. That was the difference between her and Royce. They were her comfort, her sustenance. Royce would have to settle for sleeping with cold hard cash if his success meant so much to him.

Jasmine's hypervigilance allowed her to spot him when he came down the stairs. John wasn't with him. Luckily, Royce paused with some guests, so she headed in the opposite direction. It wasn't like she didn't have plenty to do.

The waiters started to circulate throughout the ballroom with fresh trays of champagne while staff informed guests throughout the house that it was almost time for the midnight unveiling. Jasmine had been so looking forward to this part of the night. That romantic moment when masks were discarded, when the true person behind the mask was revealed.

Even though she and Royce recognized each other behind their masks, she'd still looked forward to meeting his gaze in that moment.

Now the last thing she wanted was to look at Royce without the protection of her mask hiding her expression.

She saw his sandy-blond head as he entered the ballroom. Even from this distance, she knew he was looking for her. And she couldn't handle it. She simply couldn't.

As she backed slowly away, her hand made contact with the wall behind her. That's when she realized the panel where she stood was actually the door to the private ladies' alcove. She hadn't revealed the existence of the little room to the guests. Jasmine took a quick look around to see if anyone was watching, but they'd all turned their attention to the MC preparing the crowd for the pinnacle of the evening. So she opened the door and slipped inside.

Only seconds after she'd quietly closed the door, her phone vibrated. It was her sister.

"Ivy, where are you?" she whispered frantically.

It wasn't as if there was anyone in the room to hear her, but she couldn't help it. Her rapidly beating heart felt as if it was calling out across the room. What if Royce found her here?

She wasn't sure she could face him.

"I'm so sorry, Jasmine," her sister said from the other end of the line. "I left."

"You what?"

"I left...with someone."

Even though Jasmine should have been questioning her sister or concerned for her safety, she could only respond with panic over her absence. "I need your help. Right now."

"I'm on my way to Paxton's apartment."

"What?" Oh, that was a bad idea. A very bad idea.

"I just... I want this, Jasmine."

"Please don't. I'm telling you, Ivy. This is not a good choice." Jasmine knew that for certain. Now more than ever.

"But it's my choice," Ivy said softly. "And I'm going to make it."

"Ivy!" Jasmine cried, but her sister had already hung up. "Damn it."

Why wouldn't her little sister listen to her? She was getting her own heart broken over a client right now. She knew just how dangerous those working relationships could be.

But Ivy, as the youngest, had been trying to prove she wasn't a child for a while now. This act of rebellion might end up costing her more than her job.

As the sounds of a trumpet heralded the coming of midnight in the ballroom, Jasmine quickly gathered her purse and keys, a plan forming in her mind. She'd slip from the room while everyone was distracted and make her way to her car. She could send Ivy back to Keller House for the rest of her stuff tomorrow.

Right now, she just needed out.

Away from the fairy tale she'd thought was happening and home to the day-to-day drudgery and chaos that was her life. She'd find magic again, someday, but she'd learned her lesson. Never date a client. Never get so close you think you're seeing behind the facade, only to learn the facade had been the reality all along.

Time to go.

Desperate to get away, Jasmine jerked the door open, only to find herself face-to-face with the one man she never wanted to see again. Well, maybe he wasn't the only one. She'd be happy never to see his father again, either.

"Jasmine, where have you been?" Royce's hard business tone scraped over her nerves.

"I could ask you the same thing," she choked out.

"What are you talking about?" He frowned. "I've been looking everywhere for you."

"Why?" A small spark of her normal sassiness finally made an appearance. "Are you unhappy with my service in some way?"

"What?"

She shook her head, grief overwhelming that tiny spark.

"Jasmine, what is it?"

The words simply wouldn't come. She had no idea whether to lay into him, scream and cry, or simply skulk away from the humiliation of knowing he'd lied to her. Granted, he hadn't turned into some kind of super-involved family guy. If anything, at times he'd seemed lost.

But he hadn't retreated, hadn't rejected Rosie completely. And he'd made love to Jasmine with a passion she'd never experienced before and hadn't been strictly business outside of the bedroom. Memories of him holding Rosie at the hospital, helping them get Auntie taken care of, talking about his mother's death...he'd opened himself up to her and her family.

Had the confrontation with his father washed all of that away?

I have never let anything stand in the way of my success. I'm not about to start now. No. She wasn't strong enough to find out.

Around them the crowd erupted in applause. The lights dimmed for a moment, then the orchestra struck up a lively tune. But Jasmine and Royce remained frozen in their silent battle. Without permission, Royce reached up to touch the mask she'd had made to match her dress. His other hand found the ties at the back of her head.

He was so close, his touch so intimate, that she was transported back to the night before, when he'd shown her in no uncertain terms just how much he enjoyed her. Only now, their encounter felt dirty, tainted by motives she could only guess at.

It wasn't until the strings came loose and Royce pulled the mask away that Jasmine felt the tears spill onto her cheeks. Royce's eyes widened and what looked like panic washed over his expression. But all Jasmine could feel was the humiliation of knowing she was crying over a man who would walk away from her whenever business demanded.

So she walked away first and didn't look back.

Royce looked down at the paper Matthew had handed him and cursed. Jasmine's final invoice.

She hadn't wasted any time. It had only been three days since the masquerade. Three days in which she wouldn't return his phone calls or text messages. He'd even gone by the house once. Auntie had answered the door, holding Rosie, only to tell him that Jasmine wasn't home. From her worried expression, he assumed she was telling him the truth.

But she'd also refused to tell him anything else.

He'd learned nothing about what had upset

Jasmine that night, though he suspected it had something to do with his father's visit. As far as he could tell, they hadn't spoken to each other alone. She could have overheard something, but what?

Royce was an astute businessman, but when it came to women, especially upset women, he was more than a little lost. He'd have given anything to have his mother there so he could ask her advice. Did he confront Jasmine? Leave her to stew for a while? What?

"I just don't understand, Matthew," he said, more as a way to express his frustration than anything.

"I know. She was perfect for you." As soon as the words left his mouth, Matthew must have realized what he'd said, because his assistant's eyes went wide and worried.

"You're right. She is."

Matthew started to shake his head and back away. He was probably wondering where the heck his real boss had gone.

Royce was beyond caring about keeping things professional. He ran a rough hand through his hair, no longer worried what it would look like afterward—or who might see it messed up. He was no longer the consummate professional. Jasmine had stripped the superficial facade away. "But I can't fix what's wrong until I know what it is."

Matthew studied him for a moment, then cautiously offered, "Obviously you aren't trying hard enough."

"What? I've texted, called, gone by the house."

"Come on," Matthew admonished, the tension in his body easing up some. "Where's the guy who beat out every shipping company in Savannah to get Jefferson's contract? I'm pretty sure you stepped out of your comfort zone to accomplish that."

Boy, had he. "But this is a woman."

"No different...except you might need a little more finesse. Use some of those personal negotiating techniques Jasmine taught you."

"A little more finesse, huh?"

Royce thought about that the rest of the day. Jasmine's techniques had really just been about seeing people for who they were, treating them with respect as human beings. She'd drilled that into him, but he still needed a little more work in that area.

Starting now.

Even though it was about an hour before he normally left the office, Royce headed for the door. "Take the rest of the day off, Matthew."

He had to smile at his assistant's gasp. Those words hadn't been uttered in Royce Brazier's office, well, ever.

So why was Royce grinning as he got into his car?

Today was a Thursday. Jasmine always volunteered at the mission on Thursday evenings. She had for the entire two months he'd known her. Why not use that knowledge to his advantage?

As he drove toward the mission, he experienced an unfamiliar sensation of freedom. So this was what playing hooky felt like.

Of course, it didn't hurt that he had some business to discuss with Francis Staten. Royce hadn't changed his stripes *entirely.*

He walked into the mission's large dining area just as the line was forming for dinner service. Sure enough, Jasmine stood behind the steam tables. Their eyes met across the room. He could read the jolt in her body, even from this distance.

The pull to go to her was strong. He wanted to be near her, beside her. But he had to make things right first.

So he crossed the room to find Francis, instead. The director stood with several visitors, chatting before the meal. He greeted Royce with a smile and a warm handshake. "So good to see you here."

"Thank you," Royce replied. "I wonder if you would spare me a few moments of your time."

"Absolutely." Francis said his goodbyes to the others, then gestured for Royce to follow him out of the room. "I hope this isn't bad news."

Royce was quick to reassure him. "Definitely not." But he waited until they reached Francis's office before filling him in.

"Everything has been tallied and totaled, and we had some very generous donors at the masquerade," Royce said.

"That's good," Francis said with a smile. "And I can't remember ever enjoying an evening so much. What you and Jasmine put together was pure magic."

"Yes, it was, wasn't it?" He and Jasmine were magic together, too, if only he could get her to see that.

"Now, why do the two of you both turn so solemn when I say that?" Francis's gaze was a little too astute.

And here Royce had thought he was going to be able to stick to business, at least for this part of the evening. "Just a little misunderstanding that I'm hoping to clear up."

"I hope so, too. Jasmine deserves to be happy. And so do you, young man."

"Happiness never factored into the equation for me before," Royce said with a sigh. The happiness he'd found with Jasmine would leave a hole in his life if they weren't together. *Please let me be able to fix this.*

"What about now?"

Now, Royce was determined to make Jasmine the happiest woman on earth. If he had to give up every dime to do it.

But instead of saying that, Royce simply smiled and returned to the original subject. "The truth is, we made far more than our goal at the masquerade."

"Oh?"

"It will mean you'll have more to work with when you build the men's sleeping quarters. But I have an idea I would like to propose."

Francis beamed at Royce as he explained his plan. The money he gave wasn't going into this man's pocket, yet it still made Francis happy because it meant he could help more people every day. That humbled Royce.

"There isn't enough to cover all I'm suggesting, but I'm willing to donate the additional funds myself," he said, waving away Francis's protests. "But I have a confession to make."

Francis was all ears.

"I'm going to need your help."

Thirty minutes later, Francis was more than on board.

Twenty

Jasmine watched the men approach, her mouth dry and her heart pounding. Her hands shook as she tried to maneuver the hot pan of food into the empty slot on the steam table.

They sure looked chummy.

Not that she wanted Francis to be angry at Royce. She'd deliberately told no one except her sisters about the break because the responsibility was hers. Royce had told her, warned her in many different ways, that he wasn't built for family or forever. She'd chosen to listen to her heart, instead. And she'd paid the price.

Now, part of her felt violated that he was here,

in her space, her territory. Not that she owned the mission. The feeling was ridiculous. But it was there, nonetheless.

She also needed to face the fact that she might be seeing a lot of Royce during the upcoming construction. Or maybe not. Certainly if he returned to his normal way of conducting business, it wouldn't be a problem.

He'd just put someone in charge and go on his way.

But she never would have imagined him coming to the mission of his own accord, so anything was possible. And something in his expression told her that he was going to choose a hands-off approach.

"Jasmine," Francis started, "Royce brought delightful news today."

Her smile felt unnatural, like hard plastic. But it was better than crying.

In contrast, Francis looked ecstatic. "We're not getting just one new dormitory, but two."

Shock rippled through her. "Excuse me?"

"Royce himself is donating the cost of a new women's dorm—in full. We will be able to provide better accommodations and turn the original housing into small private rooms so families can stay together while they're with us."

"Um…" Speechless didn't begin to touch it. This was a dream she and Francis had discussed for several years but they'd figured it was forever out of reach.

"And he wants you to work with him on it."

Whoa. What? "I do events, not buildings."

"But you know more than anyone what these women need," Francis pointed out. "You could offer great insight into planning and utilization of the space to meet those needs."

Why wasn't Royce saying anything?

"You two talk about it. Then come see me." Francis laid a hand on Jasmine's arm and gave her the same comforting smile he'd been offering since she first walked through the door at fifteen. "Just consider it."

Jasmine forced herself to tell the woman working next to her that she needed to take a break. Then she stripped off her gloves and headed out the back door to the small lawn where Francis maintained his beloved rose bushes. Royce could follow if he wanted.

Her thoughts whirled ninety to nothing. When

she couldn't stand the chaos anymore, she turned on him. "Seriously? What is this? Some kind of ploy?"

"Actually, it's an apology."

Surprise left Jasmine speechless for a moment. There'd been way too much that left her speechless today. She crossed her arms under her breasts and summoned the firm tone she used when the boys in the afterschool programs decided to act the fool. "Explain."

"It's an apology from me to Francis…and to you. And a decision my father will hate—so it's a win-win."

She raised a brow, completely uninterested in talking about John Nave.

Royce stepped closer. Jasmine was glad she had her arms crossed in front of her. It lessened the temptation to reach out and touch him. "It's an apology for acting out of greed."

Jasmine found herself holding her breath as he met and held her gaze. "I started all of this in an effort to make money, Jasmine. Now, on the other side of it, I realize how wrong that is. You were right. I wish I could say I did the masquerade in an effort to help people, to help the mission. But I honestly didn't care about the mission's needs."

His next step brought him just inches from her. "But I was right about one thing."

"What's that?" she whispered, then cleared her throat.

"You were the heart of all we did together."

She couldn't push him away when he leaned down to kiss her, but she couldn't pull him closer, either. The conflict inside of her refused to die.

And he refused to move away. "Now, tell me what happened, Jasmine."

This time she was silent because she wasn't sure what to say, not because of sheer stubbornness.

"I'm used to the sexy, strong woman who set me straight in her own sweet and sassy way. This silence is scary."

"Well, it's easier to be sassy when there's nothing big at stake."

"Is there something big at stake now?"

Jasmine turned away. She just couldn't bear to face his intent gaze. "Just leave it alone, Royce."

"I didn't get where I am by walking away."

That sparked her temper. "I'm not a business

deal." Her voice rose as she tossed the words back over her shoulder.

"And I'm not a robot. Next to losing my mother, nothing has impacted me like losing you."

She wanted to believe that, but she couldn't ignore what she'd heard. "Then why would you do it?"

"Jasmine, I'm afraid I need more to go on."

"I overheard you with your father, Royce!" Jasmine whirled around to confront him. "How could you shake that man's hand and say 'I have never let anything stand in the way of my success. I'm not about to start now'?"

"Because I needed to speak in a language he understood."

The confusion on his face frustrated her. She groaned, then stomped away. How could he dismiss this so easily?

"I'm going to guess from your reaction that you didn't stick around for anything further?"

This time she faced him from the safe, much more comfortable distance of a few feet. "What more could be said after that?"

"How about—I'll do whatever I can to achieve

success…but my definition of success has changed?"

His answer was so unexpected, she almost couldn't get her question out. "To what?" she whispered.

"Jasmine, you've taught me so much over the last couple of months," he said, shaking his head as if he still couldn't believe it. "Not just you, but Don and Marilyn, Dominic, your family. The problem with immersing yourself in business is that, after a while, that's all you see."

And that described the Royce she'd met that first day.

He went on, "My mother tried to warn me, but I refused to listen. I just knew that I had to prove myself, and my father's measuring stick was money."

"But you had your mother."

"I did," Royce conceded. "And I took care of her as best as I knew how. But emotionally… emotionally, Jasmine, I'm not nearly as savvy as I am at business." He stepped carefully into her personal space. "Actually, I'm in desperate need of someone to teach me what I need to know."

"Teach you?"

He nodded, but it was the look in his eyes that took her breath away. "I think it's time I conquered a new arena."

"What's that?"

"Love. Family."

Was this really happening? Jasmine was almost afraid to believe.

"Would you and Auntie and Rosie and your sisters be willing to take on a workaholic CEO and teach me how to be...human?"

Yes, this might actually be happening. "I think your mother would have liked that."

"I know she would."

With the gentlest of touches, Royce cupped his hands around Jasmine's face. As his lips touched hers, she again felt the magic of connecting with him.

After long minutes, he murmured against her lips. "I need you, Jasmine. Please help me become the man I should be. A husband. A father."

Was it possible for your heart to explode, simply from emotion? But Jasmine couldn't give in to the mushiness too fast. "On one condition."

"What's that?"

Jasmine dragged in a deep breath before she said, "That whatever we do…we do it together."

"That's a deal I'll never turn down."

* * * * *

MILLS & BOON®

Hardback – October 2017

ROMANCE

Claimed for the Leonelli Legacy	Lynne Graham
The Italian's Pregnant Prisoner	Maisey Yates
Buying His Bride of Convenience	Michelle Smart
The Tycoon's Marriage Deal	Melanie Milburne
Undone by the Billionaire Duke	Caitlin Crews
His Majesty's Temporary Bride	Annie West
Bound by the Millionaire's Ring	Dani Collins
The Virgin's Shock Baby	Heidi Rice
Whisked Away by Her Sicilian Boss	Rebecca Winters
The Sheikh's Pregnant Bride	Jessica Gilmore
A Proposal from the Italian Count	Lucy Gordon
Claiming His Secret Royal Heir	Nina Milne
Sleigh Ride with the Single Dad	Alison Roberts
A Firefighter in Her Stocking	Janice Lynn
A Christmas Miracle	Amy Andrews
Reunited with Her Surgeon Prince	Marion Lennox
Falling for Her Fake Fiancé	Sue MacKay
The Family She's Longed For	Lucy Clark
Billionaire Boss, Holiday Baby	Janice Maynard
Billionaire's Baby Bind	Katherine Garbera

MILLS & BOON®
Large Print – October 2017

ROMANCE

Sold for the Greek's Heir	Lynne Graham
The Prince's Captive Virgin	Maisey Yates
The Secret Sanchez Heir	Cathy Williams
The Prince's Nine-Month Scandal	Caitlin Crews
Her Sinful Secret	Jane Porter
The Drakon Baby Bargain	Tara Pammi
Xenakis's Convenient Bride	Dani Collins
Her Pregnancy Bombshell	Liz Fielding
Married for His Secret Heir	Jennifer Faye
Behind the Billionaire's Guarded Heart	Leah Ashton
A Marriage Worth Saving	Therese Beharrie

HISTORICAL

The Debutante's Daring Proposal	Annie Burrows
The Convenient Felstone Marriage	Jenni Fletcher
An Unexpected Countess	Laurie Benson
Claiming His Highland Bride	Terri Brisbin
Marrying the Rebellious Miss	Bronwyn Scott

MEDICAL

Their One Night Baby	Carol Marinelli
Forbidden to the Playboy Surgeon	Fiona Lowe
A Mother to Make a Family	Emily Forbes
The Nurse's Baby Secret	Janice Lynn
The Boss Who Stole Her Heart	Jennifer Taylor
Reunited by Their Pregnancy Surprise	Louisa Heaton

0917 GEN STD LP

MILLS & BOON®
Hardback – November 2017

ROMANCE

The Italian's Christmas Secret	Sharon Kendrick
A Diamond for the Sheikh's Mistress	Abby Green
The Sultan Demands His Heir	Maya Blake
Claiming His Scandalous Love-Child	Julia James
Valdez's Bartered Bride	Rachael Thomas
The Greek's Forbidden Princess	Annie West
Kidnapped for the Tycoon's Baby	Louise Fuller
A Night, A Consequence, A Vow	Angela Bissell
Christmas with Her Millionaire Boss	Barbara Wallace
Snowbound with an Heiress	Jennifer Faye
Newborn Under the Christmas Tree	Sophie Pembroke
His Mistletoe Proposal	Christy McKellen
The Spanish Duke's Holiday Proposal	Robin Gianna
The Rescue Doc's Christmas Miracle	Amalie Berlin
Christmas with Her Daredevil Doc	Kate Hardy
Their Pregnancy Gift	Kate Hardy
A Family Made at Christmas	Scarlet Wilson
Their Mistletoe Baby	Karin Baine
The Texan Takes a Wife	Charlene Sands
Twins for the Billionaire	Sarah M. Anderson

MILLS & BOON®
Large Print – November 2017

ROMANCE

The Pregnant Kavakos Bride	Sharon Kendrick
The Billionaire's Secret Princess	Caitlin Crews
Sicilian's Baby of Shame	Carol Marinelli
The Secret Kept from the Greek	Susan Stephens
A Ring to Secure His Crown	Kim Lawrence
Wedding Night with Her Enemy	Melanie Milburne
Salazar's One-Night Heir	Jennifer Hayward
The Mysterious Italian Houseguest	Scarlet Wilson
Bound to Her Greek Billionaire	Rebecca Winters
Their Baby Surprise	Katrina Cudmore
The Marriage of Inconvenience	Nina Singh

HISTORICAL

Ruined by the Reckless Viscount	Sophia James
Cinderella and the Duke	Janice Preston
A Warriner to Rescue Her	Virginia Heath
Forbidden Night with the Warrior	Michelle Willingham
The Foundling Bride	Helen Dickson

MEDICAL

Mummy, Nurse...Duchess?	Kate Hardy
Falling for the Foster Mum	Karin Baine
The Doctor and the Princess	Scarlet Wilson
Miracle for the Neurosurgeon	Lynne Marshall
English Rose for the Sicilian Doc	Annie Claydon
Engaged to the Doctor Sheikh	Meredith Webber

1017 GEN STD LP

MILLS & BOON®

Why shop at millsandboon.co.uk?

Each year, thousands of romance readers find their perfect read at millsandboon.co.uk. That's because we're passionate about bringing you the very best romantic fiction. Here are some of the advantages of shopping at www.millsandboon.co.uk:

* **Get new books first**—you'll be able to buy your favourite books one month before they hit the shops

* **Get exclusive discounts**—you'll also be able to buy our specially created monthly collections, with up to 50% off the RRP

* **Find your favourite authors**—latest news, interviews and new releases for all your favourite authors and series on our website, plus ideas for what to try next

* **Join in**—once you've bought your favourite books, don't forget to register with us to rate, review and join in the discussions

Visit **www.millsandboon.co.uk**
for all this and more today!